Ibrahim al-Koni was born in the northwest of the Sahara Desert in Libya in 1948 and learned to read and write Arabic at the age of twelve. He has been hailed as a magical realist, a Sufi fabulist, and a poetic novelist, and his more than eighty books contain mythological elements, spiritual quests, and existential questions. His books have been translated into thirty-five languages and include *Gold Dust*, *The Animist*, *The New Oasis*, *The Puppet*, and many more. Among the many literary prizes to his name, he has been awarded the Sheikh Zayed Prize for Literature and was shortlisted for the International Booker Prize. He currently lives in Spain.

Nancy Roberts is an award-winning translator of a number of Arabic novels including Salwa Bakr's *The Man from Bashmour*, for which she received a commendation in the Saif Ghobash Banipal Prize for Translation, and Ibrahim Nasrallah's *Time of White Horses*, *The Lanterns of the King of Galilee*, and *Gaza Weddings*, for which she was awarded the 2018 Sheikh Hamad Prize for Translation and International Understanding. She lives in Wheaton, Illinois.

The Night Will Have Its Say

A novel by Ibrahim al-Koni

Translated from the Arabic by
Nancy Roberts

hoopoe
AN IMPRINT OF AUC PRESS

First published in 2022 by
Hoopoe
113 Sharia Kasr el Aini, Cairo, Egypt
One Rockefeller Plaza, 10th Floor, New York, NY 10020
www.hoopoefiction.com

Hoopoe is an imprint of The American University in Cairo Press
www.aucpress.com

ISBN 978 1 649 03198 3

Library of Congress Cataloging-in-Publication Data

Names: Kūnī, Ibrāhīm, author. | Roberts, Nancy N., translator.
Title: The night will have its say / a novel by Ibrahim al-Koni ;
    translated from the Arabic by Nancy Roberts.
Identifiers: LCCN 2022005248 | ISBN 9781649031860 (paperback)
    9781649031983 (hardback)
Subjects: LCSH: Africa, North--History--647-1517--Fiction. | LCGFT:
    Historical fiction. | Novels.
Classification: LCC PJ7842.U54 K3513 2022 | DDC 892.7/36--dc23/
eng/20220204

1 2 3 4 5   26 25 24 23 22

Designed by Adam el-Sehemy

To the spirit of the intimate friend of existence,
beloved companion of the lost era, the late Fanayit al-Koni.

Woe to you, Libya! Woe to your lands, and to your waters!
Affliction shall overtake you, O daughters of the West!
You will find no escape from the throes of battle,
nor be spared the punishment of the judgment to come.
Indeed, your end will be destruction.
For you desecrated the shrine of the eternal God,
assaulting Him with your incisors of steel.
O Libya, you will see your country turn into an abode of
    the dead:
Some will perish in war, and by the will of wretched fate.
Others will be destroyed by famine and plague, consumed
    by the flames of hatred.
All of your cities and all of your lands will turn to desert.
However, a star will shine in the West,
a seer who predicts battles, famines, and deaths,
and the passing of heroes who once ruled the people.

A prophecy of the oracles of Delphi
The Sibylline Oracles, Hymn #3, stanzas 320–36

Evil consists of ten parts. Nine of them are in the East, and
one is spread among all other nations.

A saying of the Prophet Muhammad
narrated by Sufyan ibn Uyayna

A woman is neither day nor night. Rather, she is dusk. Therefore, she is a riddle.

José Ortega y Gasset, *El hombre y la gente (Man and People)*

When Hassan entered Kairouan, he rested there for some days. Then he asked its inhabitants which of the greatest kings of Africa remained, so that he could march against him and either exterminate him or see him enter Islam. So they informed him of a woman in the Aurès Mountains known as al-Kahina, or the Priestess, who was feared by all Byzantines in Africa, and obeyed by all Berbers. They said to him, "Should you kill her, all of the Maghreb will pledge you fealty, and no opposition to you will remain."

Ibn Idhari al-Marrakushi,
al-Bayan al-mughrib fi akhbar al-Andalus wa-l-Maghrib
(A History of Andalusia and the Maghreb), Book I

Never has day given way to night
Nor the stars orbited the heavens,
But to transfer power from a ruler
whose reign has given way to another.

Abu al-Atahiya (748–828 CE)

Introduction

By Nancy Roberts

SET IN SEVENTH-CENTURY NORTH Africa under the Umayyad caliphate, *The Night Will Have Its Say* is a critique of the Muslim wars of conquest in that region: their materialistic and worldly motives, the contempt shown for conquered peoples' religious beliefs and rights, and the deep-seated corruption of the Umayyad rulers. An omniscient (though not neutral!) narrator recounts events from the perspective of both the Berber peoples who resisted the Muslim invaders, and that of a faithful Muslim critical of his own history.

A number of loosely but lucidly interwoven themes run through the novel, which is interspersed with eloquent reveries whose poignant insights into the human condition imbue the book with a distinctive aura and pathos. These themes include: the blessed dignity of the female (the Berbers' ancient law taught that a woman should be the leader of the people and that the Deity should be recognized as female); the sacredness and power of language (the book commences with a conversation between two people with differing mother tongues, and is peppered throughout with statements in Amazigh and witty commentaries on the valiant efforts being expended by the rusty interpreter, while the theme of the importance of language recurs over the course of the narrative); the futility of war; the fundamental though seldom-recognized unity of all living beings and the oneness of the underlying truth expressed by all religions; the illusory nature of doctrinal certainty; the

1

folly of clinging to the letter of sacred writ rather than its spirit; the failure of religions one and all to achieve justice on Earth, and the existential questions this raises. The narrator asks: Might the realm we fear, and which we call "death," actually be the life we seek? Otherwise, why would justice be difficult, if not impossible, to achieve in this earthly realm?

Last but not least, we have the theme of day and night—reflected in the title and recurring throughout the book—symbolic of the perpetual struggle and interplay between the forces of "light" and "darkness." As the narrator reminds us, there is an inexorability to the re-emergence of darkness after light, evil after good, defeat after victory. As long as we insist on seeing our fellow creatures as a threatening Other, "the night will have its say."

The importance of this deeply poetic historical novel derives both from its linguistic beauty and from the fact that its themes are at once timeless and intensely timely. These themes speak to existential questions that human beings have faced for millennia, but which are more urgent at the present moment than ever before. We are confronted with the failure of a materialistic, culturally, and spiritually myopic, if not vacuous, mindset that places profit from fossil fuels and weapons over life itself, and the comfort of an elite few over the dignity and well-being of the many. Today, we are witnessing mass extinctions—of both plant and animal species the world over, and ancient, venerable cultures together with their languages and religions—that impoverish the vital diversity of our planet and threaten its ability to sustain life, including that of *Homo sapiens*, on an unprecedented scale.

The prolific, award-winning Libyan novelist Ibrahim al-Koni has long been passionate to speak out about what he sees as the transgressions committed against the native cultures, languages, and religions of the Berber tribes of North Africa, and the urgent need to prevent further obliteration of the irreplaceable cultural and spiritual treasures over which the threat of extinction hangs to this day. Through his writings down the decades, al-Koni has borne steady witness to truths he holds dear, seeking to right historical wrongs which, although the damage they have done can hardly be reversed, can at least be recognized and addressed through works such as this that help to set the record straight. And if, as the findings of modern physics, the rapidly accelerating pace of devastating climate change, and the power of global pandemics to bring entire societies across the globe to their knees bear eloquent witness, we are "all in this together," then to act and speak on behalf of one culture in danger of annihilation is, in a sense, to act and speak on behalf of us all.

I encourage readers to refer to the "Notes" and "Key Terms" sections at the back of the book for explanations of particular words and expressions, and for background information on the various historical figures, events, and locations referenced in the course of the novel.

1

Scripture

The Aurès Mountains, AH 78/700 CE

THE DISPUTE HAD ARISEN OVER Scripture. And if prior experience was any indication of what was to come, the parties to the dispute would be hard pressed to prevent it from ending in bloodshed.

"*Akad nakkanid anla attahlil!*" the woman declared.

"We have our own Scripture!" said the interpreter, addressing himself in Arabic to the Muslim general's envoy. The messenger sat crouched across from the imposing woman, looking as though he were watching for the chance either to lunge at her or to jump up and flee.

The woman studied her guest quizzically before adding in her lyrical tongue, "*Attahlil kud yajmad ifassan nanagh. Ilmad sinnin iha awlawan nanagh!*"

Following close on her heeds, the interpreter chanted, "Although we may no longer hold the Scripture in our hands, we have preserved it in our hearts!"

The guest scrutinized his hostess with an expression that betrayed an impatience ill befitting of his station as an envoy.

Meanwhile, the woman chanted, "*Bashshan attahlil nanagh yazzar!*"

Hastening to convey the message to the venerable courier, the interpreter intoned, "Besides, our Scripture preceded yours!"

The guest's features trembled.

"That may be so," he said after looking away momen-
tarily. "However, the last word spoken by God dwells in the
last religion to be revealed, which means that the last religion
revealed abrogates what came before it."

Speaking in his melodic gibberish, the interpreter conveyed
the argument to the majestic woman, who leaned toward him lest
she miss the slightest point in the troublesome messenger's logic.
After all, she was certain that, should they be misunderstood,
his words had the potential to exacerbate this fateful conflict, an
eventuality that would lead inevitably to bloodshed that might
well sweep her people away as had happened in the days of yore
with Jugurtha, or in the more recent past with Kusaila.

Her body garbed in black and her soul in mystery, the
majestic woman retreated into a prolonged silence. Escaping
the confines of the place, she roamed freely in the gracious
open spaces that lay beyond the impregnable fortress walls. It
was as though she were searching in the desert expanse for a
prophecy. At length, she chanted as she was wont to do in her
eerie-sounding gibberish, "*Anhi nanagh yanna, 'Awkasad itasam-
maskaland annamusnak sannamus hadn!*'"

Rushing to convey the proclamation to the one who
himself had come to deliver a proclamation, the interpreter
intoned, "Our Scripture commands us, saying, 'Beware of
replacing one religion with another!'"

There ensued another long silence during which the
interlocutors sat solemnly, wordlessly searching one another's
features for clarity.

Putting an end at last to the muffled contest of words,
the guest queried, "What harm would it do Her Majesty to
recite two confessions[1] which, simple though they are, hold the
power to spare both peoples the ravages of war?"

A smile of derision flickered across the stately woman's
features. From the lofty height of her throne, ensconced
within her magnificent stronghold, she stalked the scattered
remnants of a mirage still roaming the desert expanse.

Then, speaking out of her transcendent Realm, she rejoined, "*Aydagh addubigh itatnannagh annar wajjigh ihitajim awajjum ay middan wizzaranin!*"

Relaying the content of her words, the interpreter declared, "I would not hesitate to utter confessions that would so easily roll off the tongue were it not for my certainty that if such words truly spared people the ravages of war, they would have spared the heroes who went before me!"

The envoy sought clarification with a gesture. Receiving no reply from the interpreter, however, he had no choice but to replace the gesture with speech: "Of which heroes does the revered monarch speak, might I ask?"

The interpreter warbled the import of the query, whereupon the venerable dame warbled in reply, "*Tattawim awajjum ay Aksayila? Migh tattawim awajjum ay mghar in jarmat awkalammannit?*"

"Have you forgotten what you did to Kusaila?" chimed in the interpreter without delay. "Have you forgotten what you did to the ill-fated leader of the Garamantes?"

The envoy's face was darkened by a cloud of melancholy. However, he countered the anguish with a question.

"What did we do to the leader of the Garamantes?" he asked.

The interpreter took a deep breath before commencing his sing-song, and when he had finished, he drew several more breaths, then proceeded to hold them in as if he were saving them up for the next round. Meanwhile, the august dame veiled herself in speechless indignation. At last, after returning from her flight into the wilderness, she threw down the gauntlet.

"*Awadum wa sharran, yusiyawn imannit us darannit, yarmast mghar nawan walayassan, yankadas timazzujin stakuba asasinna mghar an jarmat 'mas awa'? Yannahas mghar nun: 'Awagh annin warit-namanaghghid daraban atakkid taddarad!*"

A stillness descended over the castle courtyard as the interpreter caught his breath again in preparation for the next feverish leg of the race.

"After coming to you as an old man of his own accord, the leader of the Garamantes suffered a treacherous assault by your leader, who cut off his ears with the edge of the sword. When he cried out in protest, your leader retorted, 'This is to ensure that never again will you dare take up the sword against the Arabs!'"

The mountain chain to the north exhaled chill winds, driving before them somber clouds at which the unyielding woman's features brightened. In these clouds she saw an answer to her tireless supplications in the temple after a drought that had lingered over the region for years on end.

Smiling inscrutably, she replied with a question: "*Anta akuniniyusan yayaway takuba, migh kunid attinyusan tiwayim tikubawayn?*"

The interpreter closed his eyes like someone inviting slumber. Then he reeled, imploring the words for the sought-after inspiration before intoning, "Was it he who came upon you brandishing a sword, or was it you and your company who came upon him with swords unsheathed?"

The envoy simpered, biting his lips with half-rotten teeth before murmuring, "It would be difficult to explain to you, O leader of your people, the kinds of acts that might be committed by those obsessed with what we term religious duty."

The interpreter warbled the narrative, whereupon the leader of the people sought clarification with a censorious gesture. The envoy shifted uncomfortably, the edge of his turban slipping to reveal his left temple.

Stating his intent more clearly, he said, "It was you who forced us to draw the sword in your faces by refusing to go to God's holy precinct of your own accord."

The wind whistled noisily through the trees as the interpreter intoned the translation in a melodious voice.

"*Massinagh iyan, bashshan ibraqqatan wayttakkanin ijjatan!*" Her Majesty cried.

"The Deity is one," crooned the interpreter, "but the ways leading to Him are many."

Then, without giving her interlocutor a chance to respond, the woman added, *"Akkat massinagh sabaraqqa nawan, tayyamanagh nakkanid itanak sabaraqqa nanagh!"*

As the mad autumn winds sent leaves falling liberally about the castle courtyard, the interpreter stammered, "You take your path to the Deity, and allow us to take ours!"

After a momentary silence, the envoy declared, "I fear we will not be able to do that, since God has authorized us to bring the likes of you into His religion in droves. Otherwise, He would not have sent people messengers!"

A slight tremor passed over his sun-drenched face, causing his mustache to twitch visibly. He felt himself reeling once again as if he were struggling valiantly to master some suppressed emotion. The contagion spread to the bare, brawny forearms that he had wrapped around his knees.

The queenly figure intoned, *"Awasasaligh iyannin wattusimad tijmayam danagh massinagh, bashshan tusamad ful ayyattajarawam ammahatan!"*

The interpreter bowed his head so low that his veil touched his lap as he struggled mightily to recover his store of a language whose fields he had once roamed with ease. After joining Kusaila's ranks, he had fallen into the hands of the invading army and had lived among them for years. Yet now he found himself straining over every word and breaking his spirit at every turn. In order to pick up that subtle, magical tone, bathed in the breaths of the Unknown, he now had to go against the grain. This tone, which had been mastered by those who chanted their poignant, mournful hymns in the vastness of sacred places of worship, was one the interpreter felt helpless to master himself. However, when the spirit of chivalry is quickened in the lowly muscle to which we refer as the tongue, then conveyed to those of another tongue without losing its innocence, it is transformed by the lords of verse into an ode through which generation upon generation can embrace the legacy of its timeless precepts.

9

At last he crooned, "I have been told that you come to our lands, not in search of the One worthy of worship but rather in search of the trifles of this decaying realm."

Then, without waiting for her guest's response, Dahiya added at once, "*Urgh!*"

"Gold!" cried the interpreter, repeating the word enthusiastically after her, like a pupil reciting a lesson.

"*Innar attajmim danagh hawanatnakaf bannan, idid yaru najmay itiyawayan dagh kallan nanagh, idid tittirat tshadat aymus!*"

"If you had requested it of us, we would have brought it to you free of charge. We have long been in search of a way to be rid of its evil, since according to our way of thinking, it brings bad luck!"

"*Idid innar tassanam sawayn, waritagharim aysikilan atawadimad ikallan nanagh ful hanaghtanaghim!*"

"If you had only told us, you could have spared yourselves the hardships of the journey rather than coming to kill us for it!" echoed the interpreter.

She fell silent, lost in pursuit of the final remains of the mirage as it wandered across the plain, immersing the flora in its resplendence, breathing into every plant so that out of its humble dimensions there emerged a gauzy apparition that grew larger and lengthier, writhing as if in outpourings of agony. Then she gave an ambiguous smile.

"*Amghar nawan wasajannin hassan, ma yamus dagh middan ma turadin?*"

As the interpreter made ready to speak, he felt his throat tighten with grief. Without knowing why, he felt overwhelmed with pity for this messenger, and for all messengers. Perhaps it was because they belonged to a class of people who were meant to come bearing sacred tomes but instead had been destined for ceaseless interrogation. Worse still, they had sometimes paid with their lives for the whims and caprices of those in power when they failed to come up with the right argument under questioning.

Realizing that his pity for this messenger was actually pity for himself, the interpreter labored to shake off the feeling of distress. After all, the two men shared equally in the ordeal of delivering a message that each of them was obliged to bring safely to shore. Even after reaching land, they were both surrounded by perils at every turn. Yet there was no escaping the burden to be borne, no matter the cost. It was their unborn child, and what is an unborn child but the meaning of the existence of all who travel the path of this ephemeral realm?

"Your leader known as Hassan: What kind of a person do you think him to be?"

The envoy hesitated. Appearing distraught, he pursed his lips for a time, scratching his scrawny beard with his forefinger. Responding at last, he offered, "Suffice it to say that he is an individual who fears God!"

The interpreter likewise hesitated before passing on the message. He then exhaled liberally as though heaving a sigh of relief after a long race.

As if she were noticing the interpreter for the first time, the venerable ruler cast him a curious glance. Then, directing her gaze into the distance, she intoned, "*Ghurangh tara namassinagh tuf tukasda an massinagh!*"

Lagging once more, the interpreter swallowed his saliva with difficulty before speaking: "In our belief, the Deity is to be loved, not feared!"

A pallor came over the envoy's features. He stroked his sparse beard with a right hand rendered rough and dry by the harsh desert air. Appearing comical, he fidgeted as though to fight off a sense of embarrassment until his tongue came to his rescue.

"May Her Majesty forgive me if I should blaspheme in her presence. Being only a courier with a proclamation to deliver, I am not authorized to issue formal opinions on religious matters."

As the interpreter conveyed his message to her ears, the awe-inspiring woman kept her eyes fixed on the courier, as though attempting to discern in his facial expression what his tongue had withheld. Then she grew so still it was as though she had absented herself.

Meanwhile, the frigid north winds morphed into a barbaric storm whose ominous clouds began pelting the place with heavy, profuse drops as violent and hostile as slaps to the face. Rather than yielding to Nature's will, however, the majestic ruler did not budge from where she sat.

Unperturbed, she said, "*Ariqqi ihitsasalad awayjanna attahlil nawan ful . . . ful tunti!*"

After fighting back a violent coughing spell, the interpreter rasped, "I want you to tell me what your Scripture says about . . . about women!"

She followed her request with a mischievous if muffled laugh, at which her ample bosom shook.

2

Béjaïa

SHE SECLUDED HERSELF IN THE fortress, which overlooked a gorge through which a river flowed. Scattered stone dwellings—some huddled close together, others amply spaced—clung to the foothills of the mountain chain as far as the eye could see. Some of them had insinuated themselves among pine groves, while others ventured out from beneath the trees' protective cover.

A short distance from the fortress stood the temple. Its solid, defiant stone walls had withstood the ravages of time, which lent the edifice a magical, mysterious aura, and as ruins are wont to do, aroused a subtle madness. The temple's façade was dominated by the sign of the Goddess Tanit, embodied in the solemn trinity, together with an inscription in the people's ancient alphabet which read, *Ayyuhanni amghar yansan, awrihanni abrad yujjan*, or, "The elder sees when slumbering what the youth fails to see when awake." It was a tribute to the authority of wisdom which, in the people's ancient law, had ever and always been associated with vision.

Crooked paths radiated in all directions from the site of the temple like mischievous wrinkles. Running in multitudes through the foothills' sown fields, the paths led to clusters of buildings here and there. Carved into the body of the mountainous expanse, some paths had worn grooves so deep as to form veritable caves, at whose ancient entrances stood various sorts of walls—some in disrepair, others restored—as if to conceal them from passersby.

In the lowlands off the mountain's eastern flank, the river changed course, forking and heading toward the broad expanse. After flowing exuberantly apart in petulant zigzags, the two forks would approach each other anew for a time, forming little islands, then parting once more in their shared sport to make way for terra firma which, clothed in green fields and various types of trees, would prevail for some distance. Then the two watery tongues would lick away a new and growing share of the dry land until, in a charming playfulness, they closed their eyes to their short-lived feud and fused in an intimate embrace before taking up the dispute still again. Their urgent march carried on as far as the eye could see, until they were swallowed up by the arch of the horizon on the arduous road to the Mother, the distant sea.

From her swing suspended between earth and sky, Dahiya looked on with satisfaction as the flood waters caused the two forks of the river to overflow their banks, submerging the edges of the thirsty land. The sun shone brilliantly, transforming the water into paintings bursting with visions.

Having secluded herself in the heights, she remained still for a long time until, suddenly, she was convulsed with a tremor. She went on shaking as though with muffled laughter. Before long, however, what had appeared to be laughter turned into pained sobs. Every time she had such a spell, she would be choked with melancholy, and all she could do in the face of her bereavement was to burst into tears. It was as though she were borrowing the legacy of the wolf, which had made a pact with itself never to satisfy its hunger without bathing this blessing in a lengthy interlude of howling, knowing that satiety will be followed by hunger. At the same time, it pledges never to grow hungry without bathing this affliction in a lengthy interlude of laughter, knowing that hunger is bound to be followed by satiety. It was a piece of wisdom she had gleaned from the storehouse of her people, the Butur, whose men had pledged to veil themselves, not to conceal their faces, but rather out of shame at the wiles of the tongue that had once exiled them from their lost homeland, known in their language as Waw. The path of the wolf, which had been passed down to her by her maternal grandmother after her flight from her father's tribe, had remained a sacred mantra of whose meaning her life had been a faithful translation. Now that the Goddess Tanit had graced the people with years of peace—a peace which she knew to be a priceless gift of the deities and which, for this reason, would not last long—affliction loomed on the horizon.

She lay down on her mat, cloaked in the darkness of a realm in which the daylight had breathed its last and night had fallen before its time. The clouds had not only extinguished the sunlight, but had advanced to swallow up the entire mountainous expanse, enveloping it in an ominous gloom. However, the rains always compensated for the clouds' dismal forebodings.

Appealing to solitude was her virtue, since only in solitude can creatures as thirsty for prophecy as she was perceive the light that shines deep within them, thus allowing it to take over on the sun's behalf. In her seclusion she struck the flint of worlds Unseen, whose sparks enabled her to wrest the commandments from the storehouses of the Unknown and record them as revelation on the parchments of memory.

She closed her eyes, recalling her conversation with the messenger sent by the Arab commander and pondering what had been said. In the course of her inner peregrination, she held her breath while crossing one boundary after another until at last she vanished into the only dimension where, as she had always been taught, there is no need to breathe. Once there, she strove valiantly until at last the darkness lifted and the Unseen manifested Itself.

Springing to her feet, she murmured, "*Awhitukalad, Béjaïa! Tusim takunat!*"—or, as passed down to us by the recorders of history's annals and the biographies of great leaders, "Woe to you, Béjaïa! The scourge has overtaken you!"

Then, after stealing out of her cherished nest in the highest reaches of the fortress, she issued the command to set out for the East, toward the city that would suffer annihilation at her hands!

3

The Intercessor

THE AGED GUARDIAN SPOKE OF the need to consult the people about the matter of razing the unfortunate city.

Bristling, she objected with a question. "Has any ruler brought her people to victory without committing some sin against them?"

Then, in a further objection, she queried rhetorically, "Do you expect me to let the commander of the Arab army reach Béjaïa before I do? If he does, he'll enslave its inhabitants, then fortify himself against me within its walls. Would it not cause less suffering for me to reach the city before he does and liberate its people from the enslavement that awaits them? In return, all they will be asked to do is give up some worldly possessions that are nothing but refuse in the end and, if truth be told, are the shackles that bind them!"

The venerable elder, who had rocked her in his arms as an infant, proudly stood his ground, saying, "Tanit, Goddess of the Generations, has appointed no one as another's keeper. For you to drag these people to freedom against their will would be a blasphemy not only against their liberty to determine their own destiny, but against the divinity that has created human beings with this very liberty. They have the right to decide their own fate, even if that fate is slavery."

"Even scoundrels have the right to choose whatever they wish in life," she agreed. "However, those in authority have the duty to isolate such people, just as someone afflicted with the plague must be isolated lest he infect the entire community!"

She knew she would never be able to persuade him, just as he knew he would never be able to persuade her. Yet, despite this shared realization, she always sought his advice on everything. It was as though she were seeking her own approval by requesting advice from a person whom she knew to be averse to consultation, and to all commandments for that matter, and who, as a consequence, would begrudge her the advice she sought. If she had ever actually taken his advice, she would never have gone beyond infancy, and she would never have rebelled. She would never have established dominance. She would never have been victorious. Indeed, she would never have prophesied.

Questioning her assumptions, the elder asked, "Do you really think the commander of the invading armies intends to fortify himself within the walls of Béjaïa?"

It took an effort to explain the intuition-revelation she had received from the Realms of the Unseen. She argued, "Hassan is an Arab, and the Arabs, like my Butur ancestors, are nomads at heart. If I were in his position, I would go in search of the place that would ensure the safety of my troops and a reliable water supply, and there is no place near Tangiers that would be safer or have a better water supply than Béjaïa. If he has consulted his own intuition as I have, do you really think he would conclude a truce with a city like that, or simply pass it by on his way to confront me?"

"Remember," said her elderly adviser, "This delegate of the Arabs' Prophet is not a soothsayer as you are. Hence, he would not be prone to consider arguments based on intuition. As a matter of fact, he is not a representative of the Arabs' Prophet as you suppose him to be but, rather, of the Arabs' king! As such, he's someone who deals with things on the basis of reason, not intuition, or what others refer to as 'visions.'"

The old man had received her as a babe-in-arms from a messenger dispatched by her father, who, lacking the wherewithal to take care of her in his desert abode in her mother's absence, had no choice but to send her to her grandfather, who had fled years before due to a bloody dispute over leadership, seeking refuge in the mountains to the North.

As the years went by, the grandfather himself had begun relying on what she termed Intuition whenever he felt like picking a friendly quarrel with her, as he often did. Her intention now was to destroy an age-old city inhabited by people for whom walls had become a refuge, and for whom living in settled dwellings had become second nature. In an artful attempt to dissuade her of her plan, he encouraged her to rethink her position, saying, "Imagine people living their lives happily and peaceably, only to find that, without warning, some of their kin have stormed into their homes to drive them out on the pretext that they want to protect them from the woes of captivity. Don't you think that displacing them in such a way would be tantamount to taking them captive? After all, freedom imposed by force is the most grievous form of enslavement!"

In reply, she reminded him of the wars she had fought against strangers from across the seas.

"Something I learned from those wars," she said, "was that the sin of city folks lies in their overly high opinion of walls and everything having to do with urban existence. The reason is that when war breaks out, the sense of security that comes from the ability to fortify oneself behind protective walls collapses. The horror of war lies in its ability to erase borders and render walls of no effect, so that the only way to escape it is to flee. Those who so adore taking refuge behind walls cling foolishly to illusions that they know full well will not deliver them from the clutches of the enemy, while at the same time overlooking their true refuge, namely, the open country! The evidence for this truth has been plain to see since time immemorial. Think of the battles in which only those who chose to flee escaped with their lives, while those who sought refuge behind walls fell into the hands of the enemy, like the lizard that hides in its hole or behind rocks and falls prey to the hunter. If people would stop for once and allow war to speak, it would tell them that their misfortune lies in their belittlement of what they tend to view as right in peacetime—namely, moving about freely—and their disregard for the ancient law. If the lords of war realized the viperous nature of this 'genie,' they wouldn't dare release it from its bottle. For when war breaks out, nothing is sacred!"

As she did whenever she departed for Realms Unknown, she drew a curtain of obscure silence over her features. She had confessed that the intention behind her plan to raze the city was to deliver her people. What she had not confessed was that the reason for her attachment to this plan was a certain mean streak she had inherited from her desert forebears—a mean streak that her interlocutor also shared, despite the long years he had spent far from his desert home.

He also said nothing. Discerning a profound pain in his features, she maintained her silence in solidarity with his distress.

Speaking at last, he said, "What pains me is to see you, with your very own hand, searing a brand of alienation into the hearts of people who have had the good fortune to live where they do, and who cling to their walls as the only refuge they have ever known. Being uprooted from one's home is a curse for anyone. It's more than a curse, in fact. It's a kind of death. No one knows better than I do what it means to lose one's place of birth, one's refuge. It's the worst thing in the world to lose your home even if you do so voluntarily. How much worse must it be, then, to lose it against your will?"

He spoke from bitter experience, having been chosen by the Unknown for this very fate. He had found himself a victim for no reason but that he was the only son born to his tribal chieftain's sister, which had meant that, according to the people's ancient law, he alone would bear the burden of governing the tribe after the chieftain's death. This duty would fall to him, moreover, despite the fact that he himself had no inclination to take on a leadership position which he had never expected. Nor had the sons born to the chieftain's brothers, all of whom were crazed with the desire to rule, expected such a position to devolve upon him. Hence, they sought his head, foolishly imagining that the power they craved would make their dreams come true. Would that they had been delivered from the illusions that drive a man to murder his fellow man!

His willingness to relinquish the chieftainship to his cousins was insufficient, since the will of the ancient law, in their belief, superseded the will of some mortal creature, and tribal custom prevented them from recognizing his wishes. Consequently, they vied for the opportunity to do away with him even on the day when, left with no other choice, he openly repudiated his blood ties to the chieftain in a gathering of elders and dignitaries.

However, his endeavors had been to no avail. In the end, he had had no choice but to flee, so he escaped to the wilderness. His pursuers continued to press in on him until he was forced to seek protection from the Lamtuna tribes in the most distant deserts.[2] Those insistent on hunting him down persuaded a number of prudent tribesmen to send a delegation to the Lamtuna elders demanding that he be turned over to them. When the elders refused to cede to their demand, certain reprobates began beating the drums of war and mobilized cavalries to launch an attack on the Lamtuna. Seeing that war was about to break out, he persuaded the chieftains of Lamtuna to allow him to leave their territory in order to avoid bloodshed. They escorted him on horseback to their borders, whereupon he set off for the place of exile from which no one has ever returned: the North!

In the North, people were engaged in a frenzied attempt to build structures that rivaled the mountains in height. Having pieced stones together to make abodes on the foothills to protect them from cold, heat, rain, wind, and intruders, they clung to their walls until they were inseparable from their hard stones. Little did they know, until it was too late, that surrendering to life within their protective walls would deliver the death blow to the poetic muse of which they had once boasted in their places of retreat. Not content simply to withdraw, the muse stifled the dreams they had lived for—the spirit within them had rusted over!

A furtive smile flickered across Dahiya's lips, as though to signify her weariness of a story she'd heard too often. He tried to placate her with an apology, assuring her that, rather than boring her with tales she had heard so many times before, not only from him, but most certainly from strangers as well, he simply wanted to inform her of what he had concealed from her the day before. He feared being complicit in a crime against innocents whose city she intended to bring down on their heads for no reason but that the ever-adored Tanit had, for whatever cause, given her authority over them. He feared that, rather than waging war on the invaders who had come from the remotest regions of the East to destroy her, she would be aiding the enemy against the city's people.

Interrupting him, she said, "The only reason I'm allowing myself to destroy Béjaïa is that I know its people would never leave voluntarily, and that they will only do so if they see their city in ruins. Even if I told them that the commander of the Arab armies was going to enslave them and use the city as a fortress in his war against me, they would not be persuaded. By destroying the city, however, I deprive the enemy of a hiding place, and liberate its inhabitants from the captivity into which they would be certain to fall."

Scoffing once again at her argument, the old man said, "The freedom you want for these people will not be freedom in their eyes. When freedom is imposed by the edge of the sword, the right to choose is eliminated, and freedom turns to slavery. This is clear from the fact that, as you said yourself, if you asked their opinion on whether to leave the city to preserve their autonomy, they would decry the thought. Indeed, they might stone you, preferring to remain there to await their fate despite knowing the affliction it would bring. And do you know why? Because to these people, Béjaïa is not a mere city. It is not a mere refuge. It is not mere walls that protect them from enemies. Rather, first and foremost, it is their home! Do you know, as I do, what it means to lose the mystery to which the peoples of the world refer as 'a homeland'?"

He lay down before her on his back and let forth a pained, wail-like moan. Then, containing his grief, he began recalling the experience that had deprived him of the homeland, and his discovery that a person can bear all tribulations, even slavery—which, in the view of his people, was the only fate worse than death—so long as he wasn't deprived of that enigma known as the homeland.

As he lay there, he told her tearfully about all he had endured after leaving the tribe's territory. Having gone from the bliss of the desert to the world of the North, he had constructed towering buildings and mastered a variety of professions. Yet the emptiness inside him had grown steadily with every passing day. Rather than succeeding in burying it alive in some faraway place as it had buried his past, oblivion had no power over the homeland, which alone refused to be forgotten. His pain over the homeland's absence was something for which he had never found a healing balm. On the contrary, there wasn't a day when it didn't grow more acute. Everything else stored up in memory had been ravaged by forgetfulness, but the mystery of the homeland fed on the passing of the years, consigning forgetfulness to an ignominious defeat.

"You might not believe me if I told you that in my experience, the homeland ended up turning into a disease. I used to steal away to the desert to breathe the air in which I'd been bathed as an infant. Like pack animals that wallow in the mud to rid themselves of ticks, I would roll in the dirt of the homeland to slough off the 'ticks' of sedentary existence. Then I'd take that dirt back to the North, where, in my exiled existence, it was both a solace to me and a burden."

A shudder went through his gaunt frame. Then, his eyes overflowing with grief, he made a heroic effort to tell her once more that he had wanted to dissuade her from destroying Béjaïa because he did not want its people to be estranged from their homeland as he had once been from his.

"When people are estranged from their homelands, their spirits are estranged too," he rasped. "And if your spirit has been estranged, it would be easier for you not to escape from the clutches of the invaders, but to die willingly, join your ancestors where they lie, and rest with them in peace!"

As he spoke, her mind wandered far away, struggling with the visions which she termed Intuition. After roaming for some time through her Unseen worlds, she returned from her journey, only to disappoint him with the words, "I have no desire to cause you dismay, but I have no say in the matter. I am possessed by the summons that dictates its will to me."

4

The Straight Path

AFTER LEVELING BÉJAÏA, AL-KAHINA ENCAMPED for three days with her armies on the adjacent plain. As was her custom in her many wars against miscreant nations from across the sea, which, though they never ceased skirmishing with her, had never once withstood her armies, she secluded herself within her tent. There—if her troops' anecdotes were to be believed—she interrogated the ghosts of her visions, or cross-examined the spirit consort which she dubbed Intuition.

Outside the tent, disaster-stricken throngs who had lost their houses pushed and shoved, wailing and bemoaning their fate as they wandered aimlessly through the desert expanse. Indeed, some were in such despair that they called down curses on the queen at the top of their lungs. From behind her veil, she recited texts from her forebears' lost Scriptures which describe houses as the tombs of the living, and tombs as the dwellings of the dead. Then she crowned her indecipherable mutterings with curses upon the ignorant masses who insisted on dying the death of slaves inside their cherished walls rather than venturing out of their burrows into the sunlight to defend themselves in freedom.

News had reached her that Hassan ibn al-Nu'man, commander of the Arab armies, was advancing in her direction and intended to station himself in the upper regions of the valleys through which seasonal floods surged. On the fourth day, wanting to dictate a message to her opponent, she summoned the interpreter. This is what she said:

I have deemed it best to fight you, not out of a thirst for conquest, but rather, lest you mistakenly imagine that you have succeeded in deceiving me as you did the heroic Kusaila, who fell for the ruse and embraced a religion which you had not come to our land to honor. For if you had, your predecessor, Uqba ibn Nafi, would not have taken pleasure in inflicting all manner of humiliation on a man whose only crime was to have trusted you and embraced your religion, only to have you betray him and make an example of him.

Furthermore, I dare say your choice of messenger was not very wise. He proved himself far more fairminded and God-fearing than you had thought him to be, as evidenced by the fact that he was truthful with me about everything. Indeed, I am indebted to him for his candor with regard to what your Scripture says about women. If he had not said what he said, I might have relinquished some of my convictions and agreed to conclude a truce with you for a period of time. However, your ignorance of my Scripture—your ignorance and that of your angels of death—cast everything in a different light. When you go to war against a people whose Scripture you know nothing about, and which honors women, while promoting a Scripture that takes such a dim view of them—a view which the doltish messenger wasn't even ashamed to confide to me!—you commit an unforgivable error against your own rule.

How dare you come out to wage war on me, not knowing that my people's heritage holds nothing on Earth more sacred than women? How could you fail to be aware that my people view women as worthy of adoration? Indeed, our most revered Deity, whose worship has been passed down from one generation to the next, is manifested as a woman. This oversight on your part is, in my opinion, too serious to be overlooked by a truce in my territory. Do you hold me in such low regard that you deem me unqualified to lead my people in combat against invaders? Do you have the temerity to come from the ends of the earth on the pretext of guiding the disobedient to the path of certainty, when your lust for war's spoils showed me years ago who you really are?

My spies have informed me of what your king in the distant East did to the only man who dared declare rebellion against him for his blasphemy against the Deity. They have told me of how your king went to war against this man and had him put to death in the holy place of worship. He then had him beheaded and crucified, after which his body was left on public display for what seemed like an eternity, while vultures tore at his flesh to strike terror in his subjects' hearts. Do you suppose that after all this, I am going to believe that you've come out against me in order to guide me to what your clerics term "the straight path"?

5

Dervish of an Era Lost

AH 73/705 CE

THE CARAVAN HALTED ON THE outskirts of the city shortly before sundown. Dismounting from his horse, the caravan leader trilled loudly, "We'll spend the night here!"

He gazed up at the mountain peak which, tinted with the rays of the setting sun, overlooked the city. Then he ran his hands over the swords suspended on either side of his strapping frame before adding in a mocking tone, "It's bad luck to enter a city at sundown!"

Then he added in a muffled rasp, "And we wouldn't want any harm to come to our precious charge!"

Some assistants rushed to unload the camels' heavy burdens, while others sprang into action to care for the horses. However, no one rushed to release the "precious charge" from the odious shackles that encircled his wrists and ankles. The tatters he wore were truly fit for a captive. His emaciated frame was housed within a threadbare robe covered with stains and sweat that would have suited a ghost raised from a tomb. On his chest there hung a sack bound to his neck with a pair of leather straps saturated with perspiration from the long trek. The straps were stained with blood that oozed from the wound they had dug into either side of his venous neck.

Still as an idol, his head bowed over his chest, the captive remained stoically upright on the camel's back, surrendered to the shackle that bound him to the sack's hidden contents until, at long last, someone approached to kneel the animal and lower him to the ground.

"You see?" the man snarled in the captive's face. "We're kinder than Hajjaj, who gave us instructions to make you cover the distance from the Hijaz to the Levant on foot!"

He circled around the captive as he unpacked utensils and whatnot. Then, as though talking to himself, he muttered, "This is the last thing you need!"

A short man with taut muscles, his head swathed in a striped turban that revealed temples frosted with gray, he went to take care of the waterskins on the other side of the encampment, then came back to the captive, using his knee to support the weight of a sack filled with provisions.

Indirectly addressing the captive nearby, he said unsubtly, "I don't know how many times I've asked myself what it is that people these days find so appealing about fanning the flames of division!"

Drawing some kindling out of the pile of supplies, he continued, "When I heard that Hanash Sanaani had betrayed his pledge of allegiance and joined the ranks of Ibn al-Zubayr, I couldn't believe my ears!"

The caravan leader, armed to the teeth with his twin swords, voiced his agreement from the other side of the campsite. "None of us could believe it!" he echoed.

What looked like the shadow of a bitter smile flickered across the captive's face, but it quickly vanished into the pallor etched into his features by the long journey and the gloom of captivity.

His disheveled head, turbaned in a miserable piece of cloth which, by virtue of old age, sweat, and dust, had turned into a tattered rag, remained buried in his chest. He dug his knees into the pebble-strewn soil, a pleading look in his lackluster eyes as though he expected the would-be executioners parading about him to take pity on him and grace him with a drink of water.

However, the water would not be forthcoming until the sun had fully set and supper preparations had begun. After receiving the drink, he collapsed on his back to free himself from the weight of the object inside the bag. It had been suspended from his neck since the beginning of the journey, during which his only opportunities to allay his suffering had come when the caravan had been ordered to halt.

As he lay down, the bag came to rest on the ground next to him. He extended his manacled legs, his wrists caked with blood where the metal had dug into his flesh.

As he did whenever he had been separated too long from Mother Earth by necessity of travel, he rested his fettered hands on his chest in surrender, turning over to Her the reins of his existence and entering the world of dreams. Whenever he did so, Earth would rush to his rescue—protecting him, absorbing his pain, allaying his suffering, nursing and cauterizing his wounds, setting him on his feet as though born anew. Perhaps it was because, since the time he was a boy, no bed had felt softer to him than the ground. In fact, throughout the years of military expeditions in Africa, he had grown so addicted to Earth as his place of refuge that he forgot that there was something that others called a bed, something that would separate his Mother Earth from the offspring she had brought forth from Her womb. His spirit could not rest unless his body was up against Hers. If Ibn Marwan had known what Earth meant to him, he would have ordered his myrmidons to pull Earth out from under Her own feet, to eliminate her from existence just as he had ordered them to remove the head of the most virtuous human being alive!

However, the earth, which had never once let him down, not only granted him safety, but hid his secret from the angels of death that did the caliph's bidding. If they had understood that the only reason he had not yet perished in agony was the presence of earth beneath his feet—the presence of earth on Earth, if you will—they would have caused it to implode on itself, swallowing him up in the process. All he needed was the ground and a sky above it, glowing with its sun by day and twinkling with its stars by night. Everything other than these two poles was falsehood, because God had concealed within them everything that he, as a human being, might require. His task was to be content with what he truly needed, which was possible if he pondered the matter long and hard rather than blaspheming against Truth's rightful prerogative by surrendering to caprice or allowing himself to be lured into competition for a throne with the Lord of Thrones Himself.

Peace be upon Ibn al-Zubayr. Peace! He was the only one who had believed in what Hanash believed in and agreed with what he embraced. Ibn al-Zubayr had been a companion to him in Truth, and what a companion he had been! Did the angels of death, or the lord of the angels of death seated on the throne of a caliphate that had never been a true caliphate, imagine him to be anxious to cling to a world now devoid of Ibn al-Zubayr and those of his caliber, few though these had been? If so, then they were lost in ignorance. Little did they know that as he watched Ibn al-Zubayr being beheaded, he had wished Mother Earth would open up wide and take him back into Her belly! But instead he had endured the sight of the best of all people (after the Messenger of God) being put to a gruesome death, and his body made an example of, left hanging on a gibbet as a spectacle for the rabble.

Hajjaj had done these things to his companion in the love of God in order to spite Hanash Sanaani, since he knew that once Hanash was in the soldiers' grip, he would be out of Hajjaj's reach. Ibn Marwan had warned Hajjaj not to touch a hair on Hanash Sanaani's head, as he wanted him brought to Damascus alive. Hence, all the butcher had been able to do to him by way of punishment for throwing off his allegiance had been to force him to carry Ibn al-Zubayr's head in the ill-fated bag back to Damascus. Hajjaj supposed that the stench of the decomposing head would drive Hanash out of his senses halfway to his destination. What he had forgotten was that the head of Ibn al-Zubayr wasn't just any head, but a precious trust indwelt by the very spirit of God, and that its odor was not that of a lifeless corpse, but a fragrant breath exuded by the gardens of Paradise. Thus, far from driving him out of his senses, it would be to him, and to others like him, a healing balm amid the hardships of the journey.

Earth began dressing Hanash's wounds, alleviating the agonies of the journey. He gave himself over to her as he always did when he was afflicted by some torment or pelted with stones of anguish by the mortal realm.

By the time he opened his eyes, the place had been overtaken by a dusky gloom. He peered up at the stars. The earth had purged him of the aches of the mortal vessel that was his body, and the stars hastened to his aid, freeing him from the agony of loss that had dogged him since his companion's death. Indeed, they vied with one another to remind him of the nearness of the deliverance in which he would be joined with the person who, after the Messenger of God, was the dearest to all humankind. He was rapping on the doors, and nothing stood between him and the day of requital but his entrance through the city gate the following day. However, someone wakened him out of the dream to call him to supper. Declining the invitation, he told them with considerable difficulty that he wanted the earth to receive him with an empty body just as the Lord would receive him with a heart free of stain.

In return, all he got was the sarcastic remark: "And what's left of you for the earth but a bag of bones, you wretch?"

The next morning, the caravan leader gave orders for Hanash to set out on foot lest the sentries who guarded the city gates see him mounted, since they would be certain to divulge this information to Hajjaj's sleepless and ubiquitous spies.

Once in the city, he was cast into an underground chamber where he spent three nights. He was then brought out, released from his shackles, bathed, and clad in a robe fit for an audience with the Commander of the Faithful. After being passed from hand to hand for the entire day, he ended up at last before a bogeyman decked out in regal attire, complete with silk brocade and the finest fabrics saturated with gold leaf.

However, the first thing to catch his eye was not the sultan's throne but rather the precious trust he had brought with him from the Hijaz, borne on his chest like an amulet the entire length of the journey.

The head was clean-shaven as though, on the appointed day, the companion had made a point of trimming his hair because he knew that the time had come for him to meet his Lord. Consequently, the head appeared small, like that of a young child. As for the eyes, they were inhabited by a majestic, aggrieved tranquility. They also revealed a look of resignation, as if to suggest a prophecy yet to be fulfilled. It was this provocative look—in an eye that dwelt in the lost dimension, ensconced in a facial expression that was wan, absent, and indifferent (perhaps because it was no longer of this world)—that held the attention of the bogeyman perched on his throne as Hanash Sanaani was ushered in by the sentries.

The place was infused with an imposing stillness which, though it quite ill befit the supercilious character who imagined himself to possess authority on Earth, was demanded by the presence of that precious treasure.

At last the captive turned his gaze upon the opponent who occupied the seat of power before him. This was the opponent who had once also been a comrade—that is, before Fate decided to divide the two men in its game of eternal caprice.

He scrutinized the bogeyman's features, searching within "the Commander of the Faithful" for Abd al-Malik ibn Marwan, who had once shared with him Mother Earth's tender affection as they made Her their bed during their peregrinations through Africa. Together they had taught its people the religion of Truth, giving them a taste of the sweetness of the straight path before Abd al-Malik betrayed the covenant and turned away.

Weary of standing, the captive shuffled his feet. However, he would have to wait some time longer before the bogeyman emerged from his trance.

When he did emerge, he flung a question in the captive's face as though he were shooting a barrage of arrows: "Was it not you, Hanash, who foretold my ascendancy to the caliphate the year I fought with Abdullah ibn Abi Sarh over the spoils following our victory at the Battle of Jalula'?"

He searched in the darkness for the eyes of the Abd al-Malik ibn Marwan he had once known. But he found no eyes. He found no face. He found no person. All he found was a puffed-up effigy strutting about in silk brocade and gold leaf. Hence, he had no choice but to reply in the negative.

"No!" came the emphatic rejoinder.

He expelled the word as though he were casting a stone or shooting an arrow. He uttered it in condemnation, only to hear a censorious, "What?"

At that moment, the lump in his throat was dislodged. Breathing more freely now, he said, "What I mean is that when I made that prediction, it applied to someone else, to someone who had been a comrade of mine in the call to the religion of Truth. This person was also a comrade to the man whose head now stands witness to us here—he being in the Abode of Truth, and we in the Abode of Falsehood. The person about whom I made the aforementioned prediction was Abd al-Malik ibn Marwan. However, the person whom I see before me now is not Abd al-Malik ibn Marwan but, rather, His Majesty the Sultan Abd al-Malik ibn Marwan!"

The hall was engulfed in a cloud of speechless indignation. However, it was quickly dispelled when the sultan smiled, perhaps to conceal his rage. Like all rulers on whom Fortune has smiled, giving them to believe that the entire world is their possession, he seemed to suppose that in order to appease the Fortune that had thus chosen him, he had no choice but to feign tolerance toward others.

Similarly, he had no choice but to ignore the significance of what the captive had just explained to him in order to justify his next question, which was: "If you knew that the caliphate would be mine as you predicted it would be after the Battle of Jalula', then why did you spurn your allegiance to me and join forces with Ibn al-Zubayr's band of ne'er-do-wells?"

"I thought you, of all people, would know the answer to that question!"

"If I knew, I would not have ordered you alone of all your fellow hoodlums to be brought to me alive!"

After scrutinizing the bogeyman for a few moments, the captive stole a glance at the companion whose head stood at attention atop the nearby oak pillar.

Then he replied, "I followed the man whose spirit is present here, though his body is elsewhere, because I discovered that he desired God, and I abandoned you because I discovered that you were no longer yourself, having chosen this world and turned your back on God!"

Their glances locked briefly, and each of them read the thoughts and emotions expressed in the other's eyes.

"That is what I feared you would say," declared the ruler after a pause, "although I would not have expected you to reply in any other way!"

His gaze fled in the direction of the statuesque head.

Then he growled, "Do you really suppose that you, or the ghost that once inhabited this head, could have done more good for people than I have?"

The captive stared into the distance, making no reply.

Then he heard the verdict: "This place is the curse that chose me. I did not choose it. Do you want me to join you in singing the praises of the divine love after the manner of Abu Dharr, while leaving people to be exploited and made sport of by the scum of the earth? If Ibn al-Zubayr truly desired God as you claim that he did, while I desire falsehood, then why did God grant me victory over him rather than granting him victory over me?"

After a pause, the captive replied, "The Almighty surely had some wise purpose in that, just as He had a wise purpose in placing the apostate Abdullah ibn Abi Sarh in authority over us as we went about declaring the good news of his religion in Africa. However, the falsehood that the two of you hold in common is evidenced by your shameful wrangling over how to divide up the spoils after every one of your military expeditions."

Just then the chamberlain, who had led the captive in not long before, burst into the hall. Seeing the dour expression on the caliph's face as he struggled to suppress his rage, the chamberlain beat a rapid retreat.

Stealing another glance from his luxurious nest at the head that crowned the wooden post, the caliph remarked, "I'm of a mind to conclude that we're both in the right!"

"As for me," the captive objected testily, "I'll have no business claiming to be in the right until I have appeared before my Lord. Only you would dare imagine yourself to have the truth."

Interrupting as though he had wearied of the debate, the caliph asked suddenly, "What do you suppose I will do with you now, Hanash?"

After inspecting his bloody, shackle-ravaged forearms, Hanash rasped, "You can do with me whatever you wish, since whatever consolation I once found in this brief worldly existence, Ibn al-Zubayr took with him!"

The caliph smiled, and on his features there played a fleeting glimmer in which the captive recognized the Abd al-Malik he had once known—Abd al-Malik the human being, not Abd al-Malik the sultan.

A tense silence reigned until the caliph spoke again.

"Do you have some request that I might fulfill for you?" the caliph asked.

Hanash smiled bitterly. Looking over at the head that stood nearby as though in witness, he asked, "Do you want to pardon me so that you can boast of your clemency to your subjects?"

The captive's question was met by a mere, "You can think what you like."

Then, before bringing the audience to a close, Abd al-Malik leaned forward and said, "But tell me . . . when Kusaila seized Kairouan, did you not wrest the Muslim army from under the command of Zuhayr ibn Qays and beat a retreat with them towards the East rather than standing with him in the fight against the polytheists?"

Before replying, the captive took a long look at his interlocutor. Then, shifting nervously where he stood, he said, "Had I not rescued them from Zuhayr's grasp, they would have been wiped out to the last man. If you had seen them fighting like dogs over the spoils during those years, you would have disowned them just as I did. I could see that the greedier they were for booty, the more likely they were to be defeated, and the more indifferent they were to the fleeting trifles of the world, the more likely they were to achieve victory. I need not remind someone such as you how vital the leader is to whether the religion of Truth emerges triumphant. It is the leaders to whom the masses look for a model to emulate. And it was this model that I found not in Zuhayr, but in the Berber king Kusaila!"

"What is it that you saw in the wretched Kusaila, but not in the man to whom we had entrusted command of the Muslim army?"

Casting another furtive glance in the direction of the severed head, Hanash replied, "In Zuhayr I saw a man grasping for the ephemeral things of this world, and for this he was defeated, while in his opponent I saw indifference to these very things, and for this he was granted victory!"

38

Taking a deep breath, he added, "Indifference to worldly allures wasn't his only virtue. He was merciful as well."

"Merciful!" bellowed the monarch in a tone of ominous contempt.

Running his fingers over the scars on his hands, the captive replied, "The reason Kusaila defeated us and gained the upper hand over Uqba is simply that he was more compassionate than we are. This is clear from his treatment of the Muslims who remained in Kairouan. He promised them their lives and allowed them to retain their religion. He was so faithful to the covenant he had made with them, in fact, that when Zuhayr's forces attacked him after receiving the supplies you had sent after assuming the caliphate, he left the city to them. He preferred to risk his own defeat rather than violate the oath he had sworn to them. After all, he knew that these men would be swords in the hands of Zuhayr's army against his own men, and that he might well pay with his life for keeping his word. Indeed, he might not have been killed had he refused to leave Kairouan."

The caliph remarked with a sneer, "I see that you hold the polytheists in higher regard than you do the Muslims!"

The captive returned a smile. However, his was a smile of sorrow that portended tragedy, not the smile of contempt that sullied the ruler's visage.

"The first sin we committed in our war with them was to hold them in ill regard. As you know, most of them are not actually polytheists. Some of them follow the religion of Jesus, some the religion of Moses, and others the religion of their ancestors, which also enjoins the fear of God. They even speak of a holy writ of theirs which they have lost. If they had no religion, they would not hold covenants sacred, as Kusaila clearly did."

The shadow of disdain spread still further over the ruler's features. Shifting uneasily in his seat of self-importance, he whispered as though to himself rather than to his captive, "So is that why you brought my soldiers back from Africa, to join forces against me with Ibn al-Zubayr and company?"

In the eyes of the proud and legendary Hanash Sanaani there gleamed an otherworldly determination in which the solemn figure seated before him read a bald defiance of everything he had supposed to be right in his world.

When at last this gleam of determination found expression in words, he said, "To tell you the truth, I cannot help but sympathize with my enemy if I see him to be more virtuous than I, more courageous in battle, more fair-minded, more sincere in his defense of what he believes to be the truth even if I should view it as falsehood, more liberal in his giving, or more indifferent to material gain, just as I cannot help but despise myself and my fellow countrymen when I see them prone to oppress others even as they boast of the mercy embodied in their religion, quick to lose patience even as they sing the praises of magnanimity, greedy and avaricious when they of all people have most reason to spurn things which they see every day to be ephemeral and passing, and negligent of the noble ethical standards which they received by revelation at no cost to themselves!"

6

The Poet

As the two armies slept on horseback in anticipation of a morning that would decide many a fate, the poet arrived from Thouda. In his immortal ballads, the consummate bard would seek to bestow upon this epic and deadly encounter a title that befit his station as a poet, and which would be repeated after him by lovers of verse and song.

The title he had conjured for this fateful moment was "The Night when the People's Breaths Perished within Their Breasts." Everyone was on high alert as they awaited the dawn, which promised to bring with it the agonizing encounter. From sundown to sunrise, the poet circled through the ranks, intoning to the accompaniment of his lyre the heart-rending and melodious songs that would incite the soldiers to fight to the death. His words reminded them of the great good that Thouda, from which he had come, had done for the nation. For it was there that their generation had witnessed the death of the enemy of the generation. Recalling these events, he chanted:

From the unknown regions of the East
came the foe without a heart.

He came to plunder, burn, and destroy,
Descending from worlds apart.

But the valiant Kusaila hastened to the rescue,
forcing him soon to depart!

Rejoicing in his presence at that critical juncture in the nation's history, the warrior queen decided to appoint the poet her herald, the messenger who would relay her commands to the horsemen throughout her realm, delivering her instructions in verse. He would convey her intentions to her far-flung subjects, explaining what Intuition had given her to understand, or what the Realms of the Unseen had revealed about some matter of grave import.

On that night her mind found no rest. Indeed, no place on Earth could have offered her solace. Her fighting men had hastened to answer her summons from all parts of the vast homeland, which lay spread out toward the four pillars of the world. Thus, the moment she received news that the invaders' hordes had reached the opposite bank of the river's upper regions, she mounted her steed and went out to review the troops. She was accompanied on her circuit by the glorious poet of Thouda, who extolled the heroic exploits of their forebears. After chanting a lament for the land which the Realms of the Unseen had afflicted with invaders from time immemorial, he commenced his epic with the life story of Idkran, who had resisted Greek invaders on the homeland's eastern flank. He then eulogized the heroic achievements of Massinissa in the struggle against Carthage, and of the valiant Jugurtha, who had staved off Roman aggression as a lesson for generations to come. He continued circling among the troops until he had paid tribute to all their earliest champions, reminding them once again of the virtuous deeds performed in more recent memory by Kusaila in his struggle with Uqba ibn Nafi and the immortal service he had done for the people.

No less importantly, the poet recited odes to remind the warriors of the young women who awaited them, and whose fate was now a sacred trust in their hands. If they gave their all, these maidens would trill and sing sublime odes in their honor, but if they forsook the battlefield, the women would weep and wail, chanting dirges in the chains of captivity.

In conclusion, he recounted stories passed down from their ancestors that declared it better to die on the battlefield than to survive, only to be excoriated in odes composed by young women whose stinging rebukes would deal the death blow to the cowards who had turned on their heels in the midst of the fray. After all, death by the sword is an honor, but death by ode is an everlasting ignominy!

7

Phantoms

As THE POET CELEBRATED THE exploits of the oracle's Butur ancestors and chanted heartrending tunes in praise of the oracle herself, she was heading a procession of young women in a rite of propitiation before Tanit, Goddess of the Generations. Slaughtering sacrificial offerings by torch light, they chanted supplications of longing passed down from their forebears.

However, Dahiya, known also in the annals of history as Tidhit, did not forget to entreat the compassion of the Lord Amajadah, whose name translates as "the All-Sufficient," and who is spoken of in the inscriptions on what is known as the Stone of Massinissa. She also addressed her prayers to Haru ("the Eternal"), Lord of the Rains, being careful to grant him his rightful share of the repast of gratitude. After spending some time uttering incantations in the forgotten language, she entered the leather pavilion that had been erected for her on the broad plain. The pavilion was surrounded on all sides by fighters mounted on horseback, who blanketed the earth like stones as far as the eye could see.

As was her custom whenever she was about to oversee a venture of fateful proportions, she secluded herself inside the tent. No sooner had she settled herself there, however, than the chamberlain burst in, violating the sacredness of her retreat with the announcement that her two sons intended to appear before her. When her only response was to scowl in his face, he explained apologetically that they had come seeking her blessing before they embarked on an excursion from which they might never return. An excursion? What a fanciful notion! Poetry was flowing off this rogue's tongue! But in fact, who could imagine himself capable of winning a war unless he thought of death as a mere excursion, little different from a hunting trip in the wilderness?

These were the sons on whom she had wagered in carrying out her plan to overcome enmity among the world's peoples by commingling their blood. From time immemorial, her ancestors had proclaimed the wisdom of reconciliation among the races through the magical mediation of motherhood. As they saw it, women—and mothers in particular—were the sole individuals qualified to merge blood lines and to eradicate one race's urge to kill others that differ from it in complexion, belief, or custom. Like a magic talisman, woman is the sacred vessel that the Realms of the Unseen put to use to bring forth progeny that exhibit similar traits, a single temperament, and a single spirit that is harmonious, reconciled, and at peace.

This is a process which can only take place if fathers are decisively excluded from the transaction. After all, fathers are not vessels. They are not even parents. If truth be told, they are nothing but phantoms. If nations wish to recover their lost peace and return to being a single flock as they once were, fathers need to be written out of the equation.

The teachings of the ancestors—conveyed in what had been preserved of Anhi, the people's lost sacred writ—had established her faith in the importance of tracing one's lineage through the mother alone. Consequently, she thought of men as nothing but passing phantoms that come to plant seeds and then dissipate, just as the wind blows through the date groves in the spring, enabling the female palm trees to be pollinated by the male trees before passing on! The man whose loins contain the legacy to be passed down to his progeny is not so much a physical entity as a stroke of madness. Hence, tribes sin against themselves when they forget that these puffed-up creatures to which we refer as men are nothing but puppets, and that their infatuation with war and bloodshed is merely a mask behind which they hide in their claim to be entities of substance.

It was her faith in the law of the ancestors that had inspired her to snag a certain imbecilic phantom who had come from Greece beyond the sea, then couple with him so that, having pilfered from him the precious trust which the Realms of the Unseen had deposited in his loins, she could nurture it in her own flesh. The treasure she brought forth, she named Yujay, who joined Yuhal, the son she had conceived by a ghost belonging to her own people. She later lost both their fathers to war—the phantoms' favorite pursuit. The foreigner had perished at the hands of pirates in an ambush on the shores of the island of Mallorca, while the other met his end in the interminable war between her and the Romans.

When her two towering offspring came before her, the only provision she could think to recommend to them in the imminent clash was to be certain to do whatever would give the young women of the tribe reason to compose odes in their honor.

She also told them not to think of leaving this world before fulfilling their destiny. Their purpose and destiny as men, she reminded them, was to sow the seeds of her grandchildren, as the wind pollinates the great palms, as the spirit grants life as it passes!

8

Happiness

WHENEVER DAHIYA RETREATED INTO HER tent, adults would scold their rowdy children, telling them to keep their voices down, since in their belief, the mother of the people had gone into labor, as they put it, to give birth to a prophecy for them.

Not wanting to disabuse them of this idealistic notion, she had never told them that the prophecy which, in their belief, descended upon her as a revelation from heaven actually dwelt within them. It lived inside every one of them, in fact, and all they had to do to facilitate its birth was to be purified. And what would it mean for them to be "purified"? This phrase had been so misused that it had lost its true meaning. It would have been more fitting to say simply that they needed to find serenity. Serenity alone would enable each of them to interrogate the unborn offspring that slumbered in the depths of their beings.

If her people ever learned how she had discovered this repository of power within herself, they would be certain to mock her and scatter from around her. However, the reason she had concealed this information was not the fear that they would cease to follow her but, rather, her certainty that they would simply not believe her if she told them. For them to disbelieve her and her way of thinking would have been worse than for them to disperse from around her. After all, what fate could possibly be worse than that of false prophets, who lose not only their followers, but their very souls? Indeed, the curse haunts them even in their graves. Good repute is the seer's most precious treasure, and its loss is an irreparable one, since the wager, ultimately, is on the greatest prize of all: immortality!

But here also, the Fates had been bound to intervene, making use of coincidence to answer her cry for help. If even once she dared tell her people that the credit for her prophetic gift went to nothing but hunger, they would ridicule her and accuse her of blasphemy against the gods. Nevertheless, she knew deep down that this was the truth. As a little girl she had been ill treated by her evil stepmother. However, it was through this that she had discovered the blessing hidden in an experience that the foolish consider a curse: hunger. Just when the ill treatment had gone beyond all bounds and she was reeling from the hollow in the pit of her stomach, prophecy would descend upon her. It was out of the prayer niche of this majestic emptiness that her first vision emerged. She woke one morning and saw everything clearly, so clearly that she could hardly believe what she saw. Yet despite her disbelief, she delivered the news she had received to her father's wretched consort, not to spite her, but in response to an irresistible summons. Standing before her father's wife, she told her that she would be dead by nightfall. Glaring at her hatefully, the woman replied that she had no intention of dying until she had first seen her stepdaughter shrouded and lying in a grave! However, hardly had the woman uttered these words than she choked on a suspicious lump, and by sunset was lying in her own grave. When the neighbor women asked Dahiya several days later how she accounted for the prophecy, the only reply that came to her mind was a single cryptic word: "Intuition"!

It wasn't long before she'd begun to notice that the longer she went without food, the more urgent and overwhelming her intuitions became. She was so entranced by hunger that she reached the point where the very sight of food made her nauseous. As she progressed in the game of abstinence, the mysteries etched into the tablet of the future became a favorite pastime and source of entertainment, as she invested her talent in predicting the futures of those who, blinded by greed and avarice, were unable to see what awaited them. However, during this phase preceding her awakening, it wasn't so much the pastime that captivated her but rather the joy that accompanied the visions she received. True, she had initially engaged in the practice simply as a diversion. However, after going to live in her grandfather's house, diversion quickly gave way to vocation as those of high estate discovered the ammunition she had at her disposal. As she went into seclusion time and time again, she came to marvel at the evil that indwells a seemingly innocent custom—one that has been viewed as a blessing from heaven. It was like gathering around a table in celebration of a meal, only to discover that the meal is a deadly poison that blinds the fools who partake of it to their own inner secret and renders the gods unable to liberate them from the masks that render them strangers to themselves and the truth.

During her teenage years, it wasn't the prophecies that had drawn her to the experience of hunger. Rather, it was the gaiety. But was that all it had been? As a young woman, she realized that this warm sensation charged with ecstasy wasn't mere gaiety but, rather, what the elderly women of her people termed "happiness"! That's right—happiness! The longer she wallowed in the trough of hunger, the greater the share of this prize she enjoyed. In fact, she eventually arrived at a discovery that shook her to the core: namely, that the extremes of hunger gave her a feeling of such indescribable well-being that she would have preferred never to return from this magical journey. In the end, she realized that the bogeyman that everyone fears—death—is actually the pinnacle of happiness, and that death is not merely deliverance and the ultimate freedom, but happiness's last word.

She would smile to herself when she heard people reminding each other that hunger doesn't kill, since if it did, the Soothsayer Tidhit would have perished long before. If the

51

world's miserable realized what a feeling grew out of abstaining from food, they would have kicked over the tables forthwith! For what people in their limited consciousness view as weakness is, in the law of the Realms of the Unseen, the most invincible power, and what they have been accustomed to thinking of as evil—that is, extreme hunger—is, by the logic of the gods, deliverance from an incurable ailment. She didn't know exactly how to describe her experience. All she knew was that whenever she fasted to the point of near-unconsciousness, she would feel herself being beckoned into spacious Realms which she recognized as the long-lost homeland.

9

Kusaila's Ghost

Kairouan, AH 64/686 CE

As DAWN BROKE TO REVEAL a diffident firebrand on the horizon, the herald's voice rang out through the city: "Kusaila ibn Lazam is just miles away and by high noon will be beating on the city gates!"

A commotion immediately broke out among the soldiers, and confusion reigned in the city as well. Meanwhile, within the walls of the august pavilion opposite the city's west wall, the lord of fear sat up, mumbling litanies of Quranic verses and traditional prayers. Opening his eyes, he muttered, "The bloody scoundrel doesn't even want us to catch our breath!"

Beside him lay another man, who had spent the entire night bent over a copy of the Quran, whose yellowed leaves he would gather up in the lamplight whenever they fell out into his emaciated hands.

As the herald convulsed the place with his urgent announcement, he responded with the query, "And why *should* he give us time to catch our breath?"

After a pause, he added, "Did we give him time to catch his? Did we show him mercy when he fell into our hands? As I recall, Uqba (may he rest in peace) had no compunctions about humiliating him in a manner so heinous that it would not be sanctioned by any custom or religion!"

"Damn you, Hanash!" growled the other man. "You don't want to forget that incident, do you? You never tire of repeating it in our ears, with or without occasion!"

Hanash Sanaani fidgeted in his corner, saying, "I have repeated it, and I will go on repeating it, since you governors refuse to understand that we did not leave our homes and families in the East to come and humiliate people but rather to guide them aright. If Uqba had truly feared God, he would not have committed such sins against others, and God would have spared us the pain of his loss."

"The dead are held sacred even among barbarians!" blustered the man. "So how could Kusaila, who once claimed to believe in Islam, have failed to give us time to bury our dead?"

Smiling to himself, Hanash gathered up the Quran's unruly pages, visible in the lamp light as timeworn and tattered from long use. Slipping the book into a smooth leather bag, he objected, "How can you be so certain, Zuhayr, that his conversion to Islam wasn't sincere? After all, with the string of massacres he committed, Uqba did everything in his power to take that faith away from him!"

Zuhayr ibn Qays al-Balawi, who had succeeded Uqba ibn Nafi as commander of the Muslim armies, asked testily, "What are you getting at?"

"What I'm trying to say," Hanash replied evenly, "is that Kusaila still adheres to the Muslims' religion!"

Zuhayr eyed Hanash skeptically.

Then, receiving no response, he shouted, "Just tell me what you think we should do now!"

Glancing in the direction of the dawn light stealing in through the tent door, Hanash said, "After all that's happened, can you think of any way that we might save ourselves other than setting out for the East with the remaining troops?"

"That would be an act of revolt!" Zuhayr exclaimed, heaving a frustrated sigh.

"Do you see any other option for us?"

"Is there no hope of victory if we hold out?" Zuhayr queried desperately.

Answering another question with a question, Hanash challenged, "And do you intend to cast what remains of our army to perdition?"

After a pause, the commander said, "I have to go out to the troops."

Hanash eyed him curiously for a bit. Then, as if to goad him, he replied, "That's right! You've got to go out to the troops!"

The commander hesitated for some time. At length, as if summoning all his strength, he confessed, "If you want to know the truth, never have I wished you could take command on my behalf as I wish it today!"

Hanash gazed at him sadly before disappointing him with the words, "This is the one day when no one else could possibly step in on your behalf!"

The narrators of history tell us that in that ill-fated hour, as the soldiers gathered outside in the dawn's half-light and the city began rumbling with voices, Zuhayr ibn Qays al-Balawi came forward and stood before his men. However, his tongue failed him. In an attempt to overcome the awkwardness, he turned and uttered the phrase, "*Allahu akbar*—God is greater!" to commence the ritual prayer, and continued praying at length.

When at last Hanash whispered in his ear to alert him to the shortness of the time, al-Balawi had no choice but to face the people. In a speech immortalized in the annals of history in just a few short lines, he said, "O company of Muslims! God has granted your comrades martyrdom, ushering them into Paradise! And now that their search has ended, you are to follow in their footsteps."

His words were followed by a long, heavy silence which was broken at last by Hanash, who cried, "That isn't what we agreed on!"

The ranks now in an uproar, Hanash shouted at the top of his lungs, "No, by God! We reject your call! And from this moment onward you have no authority over us! The best course of action now is to escape with this band of Muslims to their home in the East!"

As voices were raised in approval, Hanash continued, "Those of you who wish to return to your home in the East, follow me!"

Zuhayr ibn Qays al-Balawi looked on in astonishment as, with Hanash Sanaani at the lead, his mighty army poured out through the gate of Kairouan in the direction of the East until, as the day fully broke, he found his feet and went scuttling after them!

10

Night and Day
Kairouan, AH 69/691 CE

A SCOUT APPROACHED THE CITY on horseback. Upon being intercepted by the herald, he dismounted, and the two men entered the gate together on foot. The herald cast the scout an inquisitive glance but said nothing. The scout gave a surreptitious smile. It was as though, by withholding the message he bore, he was deliberately provoking the herald who, though he had never once gleaned a piece of good news from a scout's lips, was burning with curiosity to hear what he had to say. After all, the tidings brought by those engaged in that occupation provided his daily bread.

After they'd walked a short distance, the horseman decided to tease the herald before delivering the news he was so anxious to hear.

"You're going to have to make the same announcement you did last time, but all you'll need to do is replace one name with another!"

"One name with another?" queried the herald.

"Yesterday you announced Kusaila's arrival to Zuhayr ibn Qays al-Balawi, and today you'll announce Zuhayr ibn Qays al-Balawi's arrival to Kusaila!"

The herald's features brightened. "Oh, I'm used to that sort of thing."

"So," the scout asked, still feeling contrary, "do you mean you're used to the irony of fate?"

"You might call it the irony of fate, or you might call it the diversion of perpetuating futility," he replied.

Scrutinizing him briefly, the scout asked, "And isn't it a diversion you grow weary of?"

"I would if it weren't for my certainty that I too am a fruit of mere diversion."

Scrutinizing him once again, the scout murmured, "We ought to learn from you, then."

"Rather, the ones who ought to learn are the leaders."

The horseman made no reply at first. A few steps later, however, he resumed, "If those in power perceived the futility exposed by your need to ceaselessly repeat the same message, they would wake up to their error and stop shedding our blood!"

As they approached the city walls, the horseman asked, "So, what do you think Kusaila is going to do?"

The glimmer of curiosity in his features now extinguished, the herald replied, "He'll have no choice but to leave the city by high noon just as al-Balawi did before him, and as those who came before him did when it was raided by their predecessors."

"How long will people go on being held hostage by these wretches?"

After a moment of silence, the herald mused, "We'll be hostages till the sun stops rising and setting, and the night is no longer followed by the day!"

11

The Covenant

Kairouan, AH 69/691 CE

THE VOICE OF THE HERALD RANG out, saying, "Zuhayr ibn Qays al-Balawi is just miles away and by high noon will be at the city gates!"

People stampeded in the market, and the alleyways were filled with the shouts of women and children. As the scout announced the news to Kusaila in his tent, he listened impassively to the proclamation as though he had been expecting it. Rising to his feet, he dismissed the scout and instructed the chamberlain to summon the elders. Then, turning toward the qibla, adjusting the turban on his head, and crossing his hands over his chest, he engrossed himself in a cryptic recitation followed by the words, "*Allahu akbar*—God is greater!" to commence the ritual prayer.

As he stood praying, chaos spread across the sprawling encampment as far as the city walls, while the elders began flocking to the pavilion. The first to arrive was a venerable old man who supported his thin frame on a crude lotus-wood cane whose stem was covered with amulets inside of leather pouches tooled with magical symbols.

Pausing at the pavilion entrance, the old man cried in a stentorian voice that was surprising for his advanced age, "If your enemies saw you, they wouldn't believe their eyes!"

After completing his prayer, Kusaila turned to his guest and said, "This people's Scripture has only confirmed my faith in the existence of the Deity I believe in. I pray in a land whose every spot is a sanctuary to me. I know this from the teachings of my ancestors passed down in the sacred Scripture Anhi. If the Arabs acted on what is taught in their Scripture, no one would go back on any promise made to them, and no one would turn away from their religion!"

"If they realized how well you think of their religion, they would not be at war with you," declared the elder.

Stepping forward and taking him by the hand, Kusaila seated the man in the center of the spacious pavilion on a mat made from the skins of wild animals.

"I fear that our elder is mistaken," he began. "They would wage war on me no matter what they happen to know about me. My war with them is not over a difference in religious belief, but, rather, over their disregard for what the religion teaches!"

"You are right!" the elderly man agreed, shaking his turbaned head in regret. "Their bloody history bears witness to the truth of your words."

Kusaila exhaled liberally.

"Oh dear elder of ours!" he went on, "If they believed in the things they said and acted on what they believed, the followers of all religions would profess their creed, and the nations of the world would bow at their feet!"

As the other leaders arrived, the elder expressed his agreement with Kusaila through a heartrending hymn. After exchanging their accustomed ceremonial greetings, the guests took their seats across from one another in the broad pavilion, and Kusaila addressed them, saying, "I have called you here today for us to exchange counsel as is our custom, as the fate of our people is in the balance. Al-Balawi has received major reinforcements from his sovereign in the East and will soon be at our gates. We have two choices before us: either we go out to meet him in the open desert, which has never failed us, or we fortify ourselves within the city walls, thereby exposing ourselves to two dangers rather than just one."

After a silence, the venerable elder said, "Pray tell us of what dangers you speak."

After scanning the gathering with his eyes, Kusaila replied, "I hope you have not forgotten that the walls within which we now fortify ourselves also enclose Muslims who profess allegiance to the enemy who now marches against us. What this means is that we cannot guarantee our safety among them, since they are certain to side with him against us!"

A murmur rippled through the council, though it was unclear to the leader whether it was a murmur of approval or condemnation.

"If you are suspicious of them," the leading elder pressed, "then why do you not expel them so as to protect us from their evil designs? If you take this course of action, they will be a burden to the enemy rather than to us!"

Those gathered murmured again, this time in palpable approval. Nevertheless, the leader's next words came as a disappointment.

"Though I say it to my sorrow," Kusaila told them, "I would not be able to expel them from the fortresses, even if in doing so, I ensured my own victory."

Hearing more murmurs go up among them, he asked, "Have you forgotten that when we entered their city, we promised them their lives? We pledged ourselves to covenants with them that we could never betray even if we wanted to."

After a lengthy debate, the chief elder cried, "This means that we must evacuate the city ourselves!"

12

The Virgins
AH 78/700 CE

IT WAS AN EPIC BATTLE in which, according to the accounts
of historians and explorers, people were in the grip of such
terror that they had wearied of life itself, yet both sides
demonstrated an endurance the likes of which had never
been witnessed before. Devouring the entire day, the deadly
conflict robbed the warriors of any sense of time as though
the battle had taken an entire epoch. So overwhelming was
the encounter that it was no longer a matter of wresting
victory or resigning oneself to defeat but, rather, a matter of sheer survival which, in the stupor of combat, had
become indistinguishable from annihilation. No one would
have survived the massacre if the aggressor had not had the
opportunity to escape, and had circumstances not dictated
his retreat. By virtue of the law of self-defense, the battle for
the side enduring the assault was a simple matter of life or
death, whereas the invader could adjust course according to
the logic of victory or defeat.

Hassan ibn al-Nuʻman's army was broken in the legendary battle in that valley which, though theretofore forgotten,
would from that day onward be forgotten no more. For the poet
who hailed from Thouda, who throughout the night extolled
the ancestors' heroic feats to whet the warriors' resolve with
his poignant ballads, and to brace the faint-hearted to perse-
vere in the face of the invaders, immortalized the site with the
title "Valley of the Virgins."

The poet found his inspiration in the elegies composed by the people's leader—Priestess Dahiya—whose exploits he extolled in verse after the enemies had fled back to the Orient. As she roamed the foothills that encircled the valley, now crimson with the blood of the wounded and slain, she kept vigil over the fallen and ensured proper care of the captives. As she did so, she recited odes from the earliest ancestors about the suffering which, in such bloody and legendary encounters, afflicts virginal maidens as it does no one else. True, mothers are bereft of their sons, and wives of their husbands, and the fires of war eat away at the very foundations of the tribe. But in the lives of young unmarried women, war inflicts a wound for which there is no balm! Although men are mere phantoms in some senses of the word, the fact remains that in the law of the tribe, the death of its men is the one truly irreparable loss, since their disappearance from the people's hills and valleys is tantamount to the spirit's exit from the body.

As twilight fell on that dreadful day, the solemn woman whose name the tribes bestowed following that event upon the greatest city in the region—Tahert ("the Lioness")— uttered no loud wails. Instead, she transformed her soft but agonized moans into hymns of bereavement. In so doing, she laid the cornerstone for the Virgins' Elegy, which would be repeated after her by generations to come. This lament would be chanted in mourning over the loss of the finest heroes the tribes had ever brought forth and in commiseration with the young maidens who had waited in vain for the victorious homecoming of their men, who had chosen to answer the call of duty even if this meant failing to keep their unspoken promise to return alive.

Trudging through the mists of that somber dusk, the poet from Thouda trailed the leader of the people in her majestic circuit among the corpses scattered across the river valley. She bent down tenderly over the injured and bleeding of all religions, to soothe their pain with her songs and nurse their wounds with her elegies. Repeating the verses that flowed from her lips, the poet would put them to music, casting them with the skill of a sorcerer into the molds of the people's traditional tunes. As he did so, aided by the rebab that hung from his neck, the words would course through the arteries of the time-honored forms to which the ancients had come to ascribe an inviolable sanctity. After all, from time immemorial—since the days when people had lost their way to the vast Realm of the deities—these forms had been the sole remaining link between the divine and the human.

So engrossed was the bard in his sacred task that he forgot he hadn't slept the night; indeed, his eyes had known no slumber since his departure from distant Thouda. Hearing the summons of the lioness, he had attached himself to a caravan heading toward her den. In so doing, he had joined horsemen coming from all directions to rescue the wounded homeland. Tanit, Goddess of the people, had answered the summons as well by enabling him to stand on the riverbank as a witness to glory. As the peoples of the world discovered long ago, every glory is destined for oblivion unless the poet, rushing to the rescue, immortalizes it in verse!

13

The Truce

UP AND DOWN THE BANKS of the ample river, and across the implacable expanse beyond the mountain chain that sallied toward the unknown northwest, agonized moans issued from the throats of wounded warriors sapped by the impossible encounter. The wounded lay next to bodies which until sunrise had been comrades, pillowing their heads on lifeless corpses which had shed not only their blood, but their spirits. Other bodies, clinging to the hostile foothills' rugged terrain, gasped for breath, begging to be thrust through with the blade of mercy. They lacked the strength to endure a battle more crushing than that of the sword, for crueler still than death is the struggle of the soul as it breathes its last. No one had emerged unscathed from this round of the conflict, the most fortunate having fallen from a deadly thrust, for they alone could no longer feel pain or the grief of loss. They alone no longer had to beg death to come to their rescue lest they be forced to expire not once, but twice and thrice.

The wounded, of course, suffered varying degrees of pain. Some of them were in such serious condition that there was no hope of recovery, while others' situations were less dire, though all of them were to be pitied. Indeed, having traveled from Thouda with his verses to alleviate the affliction being visited upon another corner of the beloved homeland, the poet had not come from a place that enjoyed peace (whose blessings the tribes only appreciated when the Realms of the Unseen afflicted them with war). Instead, the wretched quarters of Thouda had themselves only been spared disaster thanks to the tremendous sacrifices with which they had purchased deliverance from the armies of Uqba ibn Nafi some years earlier.

Indeed, the poet himself had made his share of those sacrifices and today stood witness to a new chapter in the ironic fates whose mysteries had long piqued his curiosity. Otherwise, what could he call the ability of a bogeyman such as Death to reconcile two camps that had until just the day before been mortal enemies? What was he to say of the moment when, finding themselves on the isthmus overlooking perdition, such enemies became the most intimate of friends? With his own eyes he had seen a wounded man, bracing himself against his pain, crawl over to an enemy soldier who had fared still worse. The presence of death's ghost had brought them both to their senses, enabling them to realize what madness it is to unsheathe one's weapon against one's fellow man. It is as though death revives our awareness that the presence of another human being next to us is alone capable of keeping us alive, and were it not for that presence, we would have no will to carry on!

He made his way back and forth, striving to keep pace with the leader of the people as she traversed fields strewn with bodies which, until that very morning, had been animated by giants, but which now were no more than fallen monuments. Some of them were rattling their final breaths, some enduring horrific bleeding, and still others so enervated by the ongoing contest that they had fallen to the ground unconscious and no longer knew whether they were alive or dead.

Atop the shoulders of the mountains, bolts of lightning etched their obscure riddles in the distant sky with fire-plaited scourges. Some moments later, the thunder responded with a muffled roar as though some great edifice had come tumbling down and the mountains had been cleft asunder in the light of the newborn moon.

The Priestess traversed the twilight gloom in her quest to provide solace to those who lay dying on the vast foothill plain. She was trailed by the bard, who alternately chanted the rhymed stanzas of elegy and sang the praises of the fallen horsemen. He made his way across the plain, where neither death had won the day sufficiently for it to be described as a graveyard, nor had life held sufficient sway for it to be described as a place of refuge. Life had fought valiantly to wrest a share for itself from the clutches of death, while death in its turn had struggled fearlessly to wrest its share from the clutches of life. Disguised in soldiers' armor, these two genies had striven tirelessly since early morning to achieve victory and bring the conflict to a decisive conclusion. In the end, however, they had had no choice but to settle for the division that had been their lot since all eternity, otherwise known as a truce!

14

The Lesson

IN THE DISTANCE, WHERE THE mountains alternately soared high and plunged low, the sky grew stern as hordes of clouds advanced. The moonlight was extinguished, leaving to the lightning the task of illumining the summits with its fiery lashes. After a pause, the thunder rumbled, and as it did so, the plain was overrun by waves of humanity pouring in from regions beyond. Some had come to ascertain the fates of relatives, others to tend the wounded or remove the bodies of the slain. Accompanying them were all who, possessing knowledge of the secrets of sorcery and the medicinal arts, came bearing herbs of myriad varieties.

As they swept over the valley, the earth quaked with the tumult, their arrival coinciding with the descent of the first rain.

However, the poet resolutely pursued the Priestess of the Generations, who remained engrossed in reciting her unintelligible invocations in the forgotten language of her forebears. Unflagging, she combed the fields blanketed with those who had been slain in the senseless contest. The purpose of this contest, as she had discovered long before, had never been to herd opponents in droves into the vast realms of the gods, as was claimed by the guardians of the gods' hidden intentions, but rather to quench a thirst to impose authority or seize some fleeting worldly treasure.

The aged grandfather was in the vanguard of the first group to reach the plain. The poet followed him with his eyes as he trailed some distance behind his granddaughter. The elderly man then turned aside and, after making his way across a slope carpeted with the dead and wounded from both armies, came to the edge of the shallow river, which had begun rising as the rains continued to fall. The water's tongue had begun licking at the banks, leaving an impression so deep that it was visible despite the thick darkness. The wild grasses clung to their clayish soil, which had turned to mud in some spots. Meanwhile, some of the wounded were propelled in a feverish march toward the water, where they strove to win a mouthful of the blessed spring, which had been stained, if not with their blood, then with that of their opponents, hoping against hope that the water might quell their searing pain or allay their thirst for revenge. Some of them, having succeeded at last in reaching the shallow water, buried their heads in it and gulped down draughts mingled with mosses, mud, and green dung, only to be shoved away by others out to seize their share of the prize. As if in a refusal to recognize the need for reconciliation even after the defeat of the side that had ignited the conflict, this push-and-shove to take possession of the water had turned the riverbank into the theater of a new war. In so doing, it demonstrated to both sides that the ugliness of war consists in the fact that the victor is also the vanquished, however much he may console himself with the illusion of conquest.

The wounded thus carried on with another war, whose sole objective was not to achieve power over someone else, but sheer survival. This was the work of the Realms of the Unknown, and all he could do as a poet was bend it to fit his rhymed stanzas extolling the irony of fate!

After following the old man deeper into the valley, the poet found himself witnessing a struggle that had broken out among a number of wounded soldiers. As he took a few steps closer, a wild clap of thunder was followed by a copious downpour that immediately produced a gushing torrent.

Approaching still further, he glimpsed the old man's silhouette as he used his crutch to support a wounded warrior.

"*Awh kay yuhal?* Is that you, Yuhal?" he heard the old man ask.

Clinging to the elder's frail shoulder, the ghostly figure pleaded for more time, insisting that he couldn't leave without his captive. Pausing, the elderly man asked for clarification, but the wounded man let go of his shoulder and went staggering back to the river. He fell to the ground before reaching the water's edge, which was covered with the specters of wounded men who looked in the darkness like mythical reptiles that had gone rushing off the bank and cast themselves into the deluge as though they were fleeing from some unnamed foe.

Seeing the wounded horseman getting up, the old man rushed to take his hand. Then the horseman knelt on the riverbank to extricate another wounded man who, prostrate in the mud, was straining against his wounds in an attempt to reach the water. The old man couldn't help but notice how valiantly the horseman struggled to extricate his "captive"— as he referred to him—from the muck, after which he dragged him, tripping and stumbling, a few steps across the plain.

As the old man hovered about them feeling bewildered and helpless, the place was inundated, and the upper riverbeds gushed forth with the deluge. As the water rushed to the bottom of the valley, the river rose rapidly, eating away voraciously at the banks. Before long, it had begun drawing in the corpses strewn on either side and washing downstream the pools of blood that had been shed by members of both armies, living and dead alike. When the river overflowed its banks, no longer able to contain the surge, it stole away still more of the dead, turning the flood into a carpet of bodies, a floating graveyard coursing over the torrent on its way to an unknown that would lead inevitably to a final resting place: the sea!

As for the sea, in whose belly such graveyards slumber, it eagerly snatches up new plunder. Indeed, it constantly awaits the announcements brought from the furthest reaches of the earth by the torrent, which babbles about the sacrilege that human beings insist on committing against their fellow human beings even when their intention is to do them good. Hence, the sea has a lesson to teach us, a lesson known as faith!

This is the inspiration that the poet from Thouda channeled through the arteries of his newest song about the war fought on the floodplain, about the night when he saw the old man coming to the assistance of a wounded descendent of the Buturs as he dragged his bloodied captive across the sodden lowland.

15

The Captives

THE PRISONER WHOM THE PRIESTESS's son claimed to have captured in the course of the epic battle—known to us from the annals of history as Khalid ibn Yazid—was not in fact the only captive of value. The following day, the enemy captives were sorted into groups. The day after that, the captives who had been wounded were separated from those who had not. On the third day, the wounded belonging to the class of notables were separated from those who belonged to the masses. When this process had been completed, certain assistants approached Dahiya's Council of Sages with a report which, according to the account provided by historians, listed eighty captives of noble descent. This astonished the Priestess, and aroused the indignation of her senior council members, one of whom remarked derisively, "If the notables who were supposed to have been the first to die in battle not only survived, but even escaped injury, what wonder is it that the invading army suffered such an ignominious defeat?!"

After all, it was stated in their law that being of pure stock was cause to be placed on the front lines, not in the rear guard.

Soon thereafter, another council member remarked, "The army was defeated because its notables stood where their commander stood, as evidenced by the fact that he did not die, nor was he wounded or taken captive. Hence, he betrayed not only his army, but the notables of his people."

Then one of the guardians entrusted with preserving their ancient law rose and declared, "No good can come from a captive, and the reason for this has never been a secret to anyone. For if these captives were truly the best of their tribe, they would either be dead or, at the very least, among the wounded. Hence, the most prudent course would be to rid ourselves of them as soon as possible."

A dispute then broke out over how to dispose of the captives. Someone suggested that they be put to work as builders, shepherds, and tillers of the land. However, another objected to the proposal, arguing that strenuous undertakings such as these might suit captives who were commoners, but that elites could never be depended on to perform tasks relating to agriculture, animal husbandry, or construction, since folks of their ilk had never mastered anything in their lives. It would be simpler, he continued, if a decision was made to dispose of the captives by leaving them to their own devices. When the Priestess asked what was meant by leaving the captives to their own devices, the miscreant's reply was that it meant simply releasing them!

At this point, an entire contingent of those gathered cried out in condemnation. Its eldest member argued, "We have not made all these heavy sacrifices, including the loss of our tribe's choicest horsemen, simply to turn around and release the notables of an army that committed aggression against us!"

The majority of those in attendance applauded this line of reasoning. However, the approval was short-lived, since new doubts were voiced by a certain sly fox, who offered, "If we think we need to keep this band of strangers who know how to do nothing but eat, chatter, and sleep like all the groups on whom the worlds' peoples confer sham titles such as 'notables,' '*sherifs*,' and the like, we will only be imposing an additional burden on ourselves—as if this war hadn't imposed enough burdens on us already!"

A clamorous dispute went on for some time before some-one else suggested shrewdly, "We could make use of this mighty army of eighty luminaries to make a name for our-selves that would echo down the generations. We would be the envy of the world for all eternity!"

Those gathered held their breath in awed anticipation of the auspicious plan which promised to secure them a mirac-ulous renown that even their acts of heroism could not have wrested from Fate's begrudging hands!

However, the sly fox who had promised the miracle retreated into silence as though he were urging them to dis-cern his insight by intuition. When they were unable to solve the riddle, he said tersely, "We must present them to their sov-ereign as a gift!"

At first, silence reigned, though voices of disapproval were quick to follow.

The man defended his proposal, saying, "Wisdom lies not in seizing the spoils but rather in voluntarily relinquish-ing them. After all, we only lose what we have won, and we only truly win what we have given away. As the victors, we have no choice but to send the captives back to their fugitive commander together with a parchment inscribed with the exhortation, 'Asaruf astaddubid—Whenever possible, pardon.'"

The gathering rumbled with approving murmurs. How-ever, the lordly woman overseeing the assembly stopped them to request an exception—that she be allowed to keep her son Yuhal's captive, known as Khalid ibn Yazid. She said she had had a vision in her sleep urging her to adopt him as her son, and she was inclined to obey.

16

The Message

AN INQUIRY REVEALED THAT THE Arab soldier had not been taken captive because he surrendered but, rather, because his sword had broken. This is what Yuhal had confessed to al-Kahina when she questioned him several days later. He had put the sword down and held his Scripture in Yuhal's face instead. His Scripture? Yes! Yuhal said he had learned from companions of his belonging to the tribe of Bani Ibran in Thouda that if the Arabs sought peace, they would raise their Scripture over their heads. In this respect they resembled their kinsmen the Hebrews, who also had the custom of lifting their Scripture as a banner in wartime when they wanted to put an end to the bloodshed.

However, when she inquired of Khalid ibn Yazid, he explained that he had not done this because he was inclined toward peace but, rather, because it was the only thing he had to shield himself from a sword thrust! He had never actually imagined that his Scripture could offer him physical protection. Rather, he had been carrying it in his sheath as an amulet to guard his soul, only to find himself using it to shield his body as well!

With the interpreter's assistance, he went on to tell her how he had opposed his father on the odious matter of war. He told her that since childhood he'd been taken by a fascination with books. However, his father had stubbornly resisted, reminding him that they belonged to a desert nation for whom war was the key to the gates of Paradise.

He had told his son, "You can make a profession of books or do whatever you wish with yourself, but only after you have succeeded in deciphering the symbols of war!"

He had not been persuaded by the logic offered by his father—who viewed war as a pillar of the religion on a par with fasting, ritual prayer, and making the pilgrimage to the House of God in Mecca. On the contrary, he was convinced that a faith extracted at swordpoint would always be a sham compared to a faith that comes in response to the Scripture. Similarly, he felt certain that what had protected him from Yuhal's sword on that day couldn't possibly have been the words written in the Scripture, nor even its physical pages, but, rather, the spiritual Word of God that indwelt its essence.

In the end, Khalid confessed to al-Kahina that he had not joined Ibn al-Nu'man's travel party voluntarily but rather in a concession to the wishes of fathers who believed that swords alone could open the nations' hearts to the one panacea that would purge their souls of error, namely, faith in the one and only God. It was clear to him that many a nation before them had believed in the one true God, yet without appealing to the language of force to impose their certainty by bloodshed on the rest of the world.

After listening to him attentively, the Seer asked him if he could teach her Arabic.

When he inquired as to why she needed to learn it, she replied, "I want to be able to read the Scripture that has prompted people to leave their homelands, families, and communities and set out for other lands, determined never to return without having imposed its message on these lands' inhabitants."

17

The Lioness

ON THE DAY WHEN TIDHIT, bearing her house on her back in keeping with the law of her nomadic Butur ancestors, set out after the wounded warrior Hassan ibn al-Nu'man with her entire army, the poet hastened to join the procession, on his lips words of praise for the Seer of the Generation, and in his heart, the truth that the ancestors had deposited from all eternity within the city's name—Tahurt. He alone had been authorized to give voice to the mortal distress that lay heavy on her chest and paralyzed her tongue. What's more, he alone knew the story about her of which she herself was ignorant, or perhaps feigned ignorance, either out of disdain or in response to a will greater than her own, otherwise known as forgetfulness!

When, surrounded by temple custodians, ladies-in-waiting, and army commanders, the Seer visited the shrine of the Goddess Tanit to bathe its altar in the blood of sacrifices in gratitude for the victory she had been granted, the poet joined in the solemn rites. While reciting the prayers, he was swept up with the other worshipers in the feverish, mournful chanting, thence to emerge as a phantom imbued with inspiration. As the solemn procession set out toward the East, the poet repeated a hymn borrowed from an astute proverb derived from the teachings of the ancients. Such teachings warned against making light of a lion one has wounded, then left alive, or a viper one has injured without cutting off its head. For wherever he goes, a wounded enemy will never rest until he has settled the score. Hassan ibn al-Nu'man was such a foe, a lion wounded and bleeding whose eastward flight had only one purpose: to find a lair in which to nurse his wounds before retracing his steps and taking revenge. Defeat is the one unforgivable offense. Consequently, the Court of Eternity has ruled that whoever wishes to escape such a backlash must pursue the enemy and deal him the death blow before he finds himself a resting place in which to catch his breath.

The poet chanted this message of worldly wisdom, urging the fainthearted to be vigilant and inspiring the heroic to bring to completion what they had been unable to accomplish in Wadi al-Adhara—the Valley of the Virgins. Then, as the procession was about the enter Tahurt, the city of many ages—whose name, in an allusion to its impregnability, means "the door" or "the gate" in the language of its people—he went on to sing of the history of this name, which since time immemorial had shielded the city like an amulet from the greed of hostile invaders. But now and from this day onward, it would relinquish its age-old appellation and replace it with the name Tahert—"the Lioness"—now that the glorious Seer had granted it good fortune by descending upon its vast expanses as an invincible guest and achieving glory for the city and all generations to come. While the name Tahurt—"the Gate"—had long provided security for the city's inhabitants when they aspired to nothing but self-defense, the name Tahert—"the Lioness"—was the auspicious omen that would usher them out of an era of defense into one of offense.

Poets of that day could only win their tribes' adulation by producing something that dazzled their listeners or, at the very least, piqued their curiosity. Accordingly, the bard from Thouda astonished the people with something that had theretofore been concealed from them. To wit, his compositions revealed that Tahert ("the Lioness") was the secret name their Seer had obtained at birth. The name had remained concealed in keeping with the customs of the nomadic Butur tribes, who believed that the pseudonym a person was given at birth represented the actions its bearer would undertake. It inscribed person's life story on their soul, while at the same time serving as a protective amulet to shield the hero from evil until such time as they were able to weave the fabric of the name that they would obtain on merit. Only those exceptional souls who had been chosen by the Realms of the Unseen to be messengers, sages, or champions could achieve the qualities of both the secret, magical name given freely at birth, and the other name acquired by the force of their character. When this took place, the two qualities would be smelted into an alloy that would undergird the Throne of Chosenness!

At birth, the Seer's family had given her the pseudonym Tidhit—"Sandy Earth"—as a kind of camouflage. When the Arabs came, they replaced the name with Dahiya ("the Cunning One"), particularly after recognizing her resourcefulness. However, once cunning, which entails the good sense and flexibility required to negotiate rough, sandy terrain (Tidhit) was combined with the strength of the Lioness (Tahert) and her ferocity in defense of her cubs, the will of the Realms of the Unseen would be fully revealed.

These are the things about which the poet sang in verse as the procession entered Tahurt—"The Gate"—which had now spurned its earlier name, presenting it as an offering in happy anticipation of the arrival of Tahert—"the Lioness"— in her abode. On that day, the city stood tall as a vanguard, upheld by the spirit of the Goddess in the eastward campaign.

18

Certainty

AS NIGHT FELL, AL-KAHINA SECLUDED herself, speaking in private with the stars suspended in a cloudless sky. The earth had no reason to lament the moon's absence, since the dazzling radiance so liberally bestowed by the stars—as radiant as the benefactions of a full moon—rendered the darkness of no effect. Only in the desert night do the stars so generously confer the resplendence of their storehouse of lights, enabling the lower realms to dispense with moons in their vast expanses. Long captivated by the cryptic babblings of these heavenly lamps, she devoted herself to conversing with them whenever the opportunity arose, intent on deciphering in their gleam the messages being sent by the hidden Realm. This was the Realm which, having made a covenant with her, had granted her the vision in which she saw her stepmother shrouded atop a leather mat. Her open, bulging eyes had been swathed in a ghastly whiteness as though they were staring into nothingness, or, possibly, at the specter of the encounter she had long dreaded, her lips ringed with thick foam as she struggled to cling to the breaths that stood between her and her demise.

These ever-vigilant, celestial eyes had messages to declare in their onward march, messages that needed to be interpreted aright: What, for example, was being proclaimed by that bright star whose only concern was to blink in the night sky? It was voicing a prophecy which, translated, said, "Take cover! Take cover!" as if alerting Earth's inhabitants to the approach of the winter frost. What about that other star, the one ascending over the horizon and awash in the glow of twilight? It was warning of the winds about to blow. What news was borne by the tight assembly over yonder, the one gathered in on itself like a band of criminals hatching a sinister midnight plot? It was simply searching for a way to inform people that the fruits atop the date palms' crowns had ripened.

To the ordinary inhabitants of the lower spheres, the assemblies of the stars are the interpreters of the seasons. But to the tribes' spiritual elites, they are the interpreters of Fate, and in this capacity had urged her to set out in pursuit of Ibn al-Nu'man. In so doing, she would be seeking the stars' blessing, since they themselves had adopted outer space as their sphere of pursuit, racing through their cosmic Realms in hopes of being pursued themselves. After all, what does it mean to exist if one does not pursue, if one does not engage in the chase? Far better to content oneself with the pursuit than to capture what one pursues, since felling one's prey brings the chase to an end.

She had been told that there was no greater foolishness than to tighten the noose around a wounded lion, which is what her opponent was. However, she merely smiled knowingly at the notables who had spoken thus to her. They were misjudging her if they imagined that her goal was to win her prey. Rather, the objective of the chase was the chase itself, the pleasure of the chase, the perception of the chase as an enjoyable excursion. Only the fool would sacrifice the enjoyment afforded by an excursion by seeking to capture a prey he imagines to be the prize, forgetting that in possession of the desired object lies death. As for her, she was too astute to seek to capture or even close in on him. Otherwise, she would not have been dubbed Dahiya, "the Cunning One."

She also had another reason for not striving to capture Ibn al-Nu'man. It was a reason that, having come to her through Intuition, was known to none but her. Before the stars had whispered it in her ear, she had seen it in the vision of visions. She had heard it from the voice of prophetic inspiration, which reminded her of the eternal but forgotten teaching that the fire of vision in the abodes of the West would be extinguished when a new firebrand approached on horseback from the East. After all, there is a time for everything, including prophecies and homelands. Indeed, Earth itself would change and pass away before its time unless it grew restless for renewal. The glory of mothers had now passed away, and with it the era of priestesses, to be succeeded by the era of fathers crowned by the religions of the prophets. She had no choice but to accept Ibn al-Nu'man as a message bearer specifically for her. She would thus receive him as one who had come to warn her that the time had come, because the law of the chase which had been put to use by the Realms of the Unseen against the Earth Herself still held sway, and the religion Ibn al-Nu'man had come to proclaim was Destiny's word to her.

Prolonging an era requires that one prolong the quest, prolonging the quest requires that one avoid confrontation, and avoiding confrontation requires that one keep one's distance in the chase. This was the age-old truth she had observed in the night's endless pursuit of the day, and the day's pursuit of the night. Imagine what might happen to the earth and its inhabitants were one of them to overtake the other and swallow it up!

According to the precepts of the lost law, no certainty can bear to be present in a land where some other certainty reigns. On the contrary, "certainty," which some refer to as religion, will not be content anywhere until it has stifled the old "certainty." Moreover, although the newly arrived certainty sees no conflict with the content of the certainty that preceded it, the mere fact that the earlier certainty manifests itself differently than does the new certainty is sufficient reason to accuse it of blasphemy against the Deity and, accordingly, to usurp its place in people's hearts.

Everyone sings the praises of the Deity, yet no one hesitates to kill the Deity's other servants, for the simple reason that they chant a different tune!

A new certainty holds sway until, at long last, a day comes bearing an even newer certainty which banishes its predecessor, just as the light of the newborn day banishes the darkness of a long cold night. As succeeding generations have come to see in the course of their bitter struggle against falsehood, even certainty, being composed of the same clay as its possessor, grows old and decrepit.

19

Language
Tahert, AH 89/708 CE

THE SEER KEPT VIGIL FOR some time in the fortresses of Tahert. After sending out scouts to gather information on the broken Hassan ibn al-Nu'man in his feverish eastward flight, she received news that he had set up camp in Kairouan to await the arrival of supplies from an inexhaustible repository in the East. In so doing, he was carrying on the tradition of defeated military commanders who, after getting a taste of the Western regions and their treasures, would withdraw some distance to station themselves here or there for a period of time while they regrouped and nursed their wounds. Then, when they had received more men and equipment from the abundant storehouse, they would launch another assault.

As for her, she made ready to set out from Tahert to raid the wounded lion before he could catch his breath or receive the magic charm from the unknown regions of the legendary East, where bottomless repositories sustained rulers whose greed knew no bounds. Before giving the command to set out, however, she would knit the bonds of covenant between the offspring to which she had given birth and nourished with her own blood, and the outsider she had chosen to include among her progeny. She would draw him in through an ancient rite that would render him worthy to be her son.

The longing for brotherhood that had inspired the dreams of earlier generations had revealed the failings of those who came after them. The ancients had woven the bonds of brotherhood among the age-old tribes, thereby preventing them from making a profession of war, but their successors had neglected the inherited rites of mingling bloodlines, sparking enmities among the nations and kindling the flames of wars that had brought affliction on all sides. Moreover, they had done so despite everyone's claims to embrace the earliest Scriptures' commands to foster goodwill among all. Thanks to the ancients' practice of devising ruses to lure people to live as brothers in their fellow men's territories, memorials of alliance had been erected, guaranteeing everyone the freedom to live in everyone else's lands. As a result, people would seek each other's assistance rather than taking each other's lives. But in later times, they abandoned the divinely mediated ceremonies for inviting people into each other's sacred spaces and forging covenants of solidarity. Such covenants had, like mother's milk, created brothers not by virtue of a shared womb but rather by the will of a deity who was herself a womb—indeed, the womb that had given birth to all other wombs. Motherhood is a miraculous vessel imbued with a cryptic power through which the creation was brought into existence out of nothing.

It was with these truths in mind that the Seer of the Generation addressed the son who had come to her from an eastern land inhabited by strangers who, had they not lost the ancient protective amulet[3] by which preceding generations had sought to escape annihilation at the hands of neighboring nations, would not have been strangers to her and who, had they appealed to the wisdom of generations past, would have understood themselves to be her brothers.

She had noticed long before how capably the adopted son who had entered her territory as an invader had mastered her language, while she still struggled to unlock the secrets of the Arabic tongue despite his valiant attempts to teach her. She longed to quench her thirst to read the book which, alone among the world's Scriptures, had derived its name from the very act of reading.[4] When she expressed her amazement at how quickly he had absorbed her language, he would humor her, reminding her that the credit for rapid acquisition of the tongues of the world actually goes to the lands to which these tongues belong, as though the land were the one that spoke the language and had been authorized to teach it. Indeed, it is well-nigh impossible to learn the language of a people in whose country one has not lived, since only by living there can one perform the sacred duties of allegiance to the majesty of language in its very sanctum, the site a given language has chosen as its homeland.

"You have to believe in the message the Book brought down," he explained. "And if you want the land of the Arabs to acknowledge you and open its heart to you, you'll need to go there with me. Only then will this 'strangers' tongue' roll off your tongue as it ought to."

Then he added mischievously, "Even the language's native speakers don't learn their language on their own. It's the land that teaches them. When they do learn it, they don't so much speak their own language as they babble away in the tongue of the place they call home. You'll ever succeed in learning some other people's language unless you give up your pride and exile yourself to the land whose language you intend to borrow."

20

Brotherhood

SHE PACED THE HOUSE, MAKING circles around herself, wondering whether the ancestors had sinned against Fate by continuously setting snares for this bogeyman and attempting to pull the wool over its eyes as they had done so many times. Otherwise, what was she to call their practice of giving male children slave names as a kind of "camouflage," hoping that Fate would fall for the ruse instead of snatching them away the moment they were born? Some of them had shown such contempt for this terrifying bogeyman that they had pierced their little boys' ears to make them look like girls, thinking that Fate would leave them alone as though it were some gullible child.

As for milk's sway over living creatures, she had experienced it firsthand when a certain genie had advised her to conclude a pact of brotherhood between her son Yuhal and scorpions in order to protect him from their nasty sting. After squeezing some breast milk into a container, she caught a scorpion, placed it in the milk, and left it there for three days and nights before releasing it back into the desert. Thereafter, scorpions had stopped stinging the baby boy. He could even play with them, letting them crawl over his wrists or face without doing him the slightest harm.

If mother's milk could restrain a scorpion from stinging someone, how could its power fail to forge the bonds of a covenant between two human beings?

But how could such bonds be forged between sons if the wellsprings of milk in her breasts had gone dry by virtue of her age? Might it help to pretend there was milk in them when concluding the deal the way ingenious tribeswomen pretended when they pierced their little boys' ears? After all, she had seen Fate respond favorably to such ploys as though it had a taste for lies, even though it was fully aware of the facts being concealed. Did Fate simply pretend to fall for people's ruses? Did it turn a blind eye to their transgressions, then answer their pleas while muffling a giggle, like a woman who admits to her weakness for men's sweet talk even though she knows it's nothing but lies embellished with more lies?

And what about her? She herself feared Fate and constantly sought protection against it with offerings to the Deity. She felt certain that the Goddess Tanit had assigned Fate to represent Her in carrying out Her will for humanity. Fate had served as her guardian: It had never once begrudged her a prophecy, and it had forgiven her for sins she had committed against both herself and others. How many times had she thought: What is Fate, if not the law that governs on behalf of the Goddess? A wise law that never wrongs anyone, it punishes evildoers through their own evil deeds, by the works of their own hands. It is stern, without a doubt. Nevertheless, there is a hilarity about it when it feels like making fun, as though it is proving its ability to expose what the wicked are bent on concealing.

Shrewd and knowing, Fate fulfills our wishes not because it's been taken in by our childish ruses—in fact, it finds them amusing—but out of pity for us. Yet is it mere pity? Not at all—rather, in the contest against dreams, Fate's weakness is revealed. In a confrontation with the force known as dreaming, even the Almighty Fate will raise its hands in surrender. What people most desire is something that will transform their dreams into a genuine fever, a fiery obsession that melts the iron core of the law. And when this happens, it so softens the heart of Fate that it has no choice but to do the dreams' bidding. This is what priests refer to as a miracle. Hence, they never tire of exhorting us, "Dream well, for there is nothing impossible to those who dream!"

So, she wondered: Had she herself dreamed well? All she knew was that very early in her life, she had begun dreaming of how to reinforce the pillars of brotherhood, not only among members of the human race, but between human beings and hyenas, lions, snakes, and scorpions. She had striven to bring about harmony with anything and everything that had the potential of doing harm until, over time, this dream had become an all-consuming obsession. To her sorrow, however, the only time she had succeeded in fulfilling it had been when she struck a deal with the nation of scorpions using milk squeezed from her own breast.

The dream of achieving brotherhood among fellow members of the human race had turned into a veritable malady in her life. How is it, she wondered, that human beings, who are supposed to be brothers and sisters, suddenly turn on one another? How is it that they turn into enemies, rapacious wolves, when wolves themselves have never been "wolves" to one another? After spending long years consumed by wars of self-defense against invaders who had come from across the sea, she had done everything in her power to tame their hostility and win them over as brothers. And in fact, she had succeeded in domesticating entire nations. When invaders settled in her extensive territory, she had shared her abundant wealth with them out of sheer goodwill, not under threat of the sword. Yet now she was being forced into new wars against invaders who had approached from the furthest reaches of the East. She would gladly have received them as guests to whom she begrudged nothing by way of shelter or sustenance. They could have been helpers and friends to her—and, more importantly, brothers—in her vast land!

Having failed thus far to achieve this aspiration with those in command, she had decided to conclude a pact of brotherhood between her two sons by birth and a son of enemy notables whom Fate had placed in her hands as a captive of war. The rites of brotherhood among the three young men would be on the order of a covenant sealed by the power of the breast and mediated by sacred foods.[5] The covenant would serve as a protective amulet of sorts for those of their generation, since they would now be the source of power in the days to come. As for her, there was nothing she could rely on after the sacrifices she had made over the course of a lifetime, whose bitterness had brought no regrets, and whose sweetness had engendered no illusions.

21

Love

THE BROTHERLY BOND FORMED BY nursing a child other than a woman's own is an enduring covenant. This covenant can be concluded even after the springs of milk in her nipples have dried up, and her breasts begrudge her the magic talisman that possesses this binding power. For when barley flour kneaded with amulet water—water in which magic spells written in the forgotten alphabet on snake-skin parchments have been dissolved—is exposed to moonlight for three consecutive nights, it can be used to restore the flow of the precious liquid that has been lost with the passage of time.[6]

"*Kunid dimagh tamusam anghatan*—you are now brothers!" declared the Priestess of the Generations with motherly authority. She had just completed the rites of lactation with the reverence of someone concluding a ritual prayer in the temple of the Goddess.

Old age insists on having its say against youth just as the night insists on having its say against the day. But now she, too, had had her say. She too had given voice to her mystery. Then she left them and went out to the garden. There, among the olive trees, she lingered alone as was her custom whenever she was overcome by a sudden bout of melancholy or burdened by some affliction. In recent days, melancholy seemed to have appointed itself her guardian. As for affliction, it had never left her side, its ghost shadowing her even in times of victory and good fortune. As she knew all too well, every leap is followed by a stumble, and the greatest vigilance can be rendered of no effect by a moment of heedlessness, for the night lies in wait for the day!

She rolled up her sleeves, revealing forearms that bristled with amulets concealed within leather bracelets, some of whose delicate embellishments represented the symbols of the Goddess. Others, unidentified, were written in the secret alphabet she had inherited from her ancestors. She lifted her arms over her head as if to dedicate them to a moonless sky, or to join them to the thrones of brilliant stars in whose enduring gleam she had discerned many a prophecy. After standing perfectly still for a moment, she made cryptic utterances in the forgotten language, her arms still raised like an offering suspended between heaven and earth.

The prayer wasn't a lengthy one, but she didn't return from her journey even when it had come to an end. The dream that had always haunted her had become a constant preoccupation. She had tried to dispel it by every means at her disposal. Every offering she had ever made had been a votive gift presented at the altar of dreams. What else could have prompted her to draw a man of her own race into her bedchamber, if not the call to obtain offspring from his loins? What could have prompted her to lure a stranger into her embrace if not the unshakable belief in the power of blood ties to prevent successive generations from mutual bloodshed?

It was an ideal that could never be achieved without the assistance of mothers, and this was a charge she had received as an individual mother. How much more would be required of her now that the Law had willed her to be a mother to an entire nation? The duty to protect her offspring had been hung as a weight about her neck not once, but twice. She had given voice to the mystery ever so early, perhaps as early as young childhood, during the years when she had endured such hatred at the hands of her stepmother. That malicious woman's hatred clearly lay at the root of the malady that had ravaged her throughout the years that followed, as she searched for the mysterious potion that could revive the love that had gone missing from people's hearts.

Yes, she wanted to reclaim lost love, to revive a love she thought had died. However, she did not seek to revive it in order to possess it exclusively for herself. Love would no longer be love if she acquired it for herself alone or claimed it as her personal possession; she sought it only so that she could give it away. She sought love so that it could spread everywhere, certain in her belief that as love prevailed, so would peace: peace within families, peace among tribes, and peace among nations.

Yes, if she could answer love's summons by raising its banner among tribes everywhere and receiving the invaders with a warm embrace, she would drive the last nail into war's coffin, and bloodshed would cease forevermore.

Knowing that she could only persuade others to do something if she herself set the example, she had sought to establish a tradition of fostering love through the mediation of the womb. She had coupled with a foreigner in order to pilfer from his loins a son who by virtue of the ties of blood would become a brother to the son she had conceived by a fellow countryman. Through their mutual belonging, they would conclude a covenant mediated by love—the mightiest thing in the earthly realm!

Since she had begun with herself, other tribeswomen followed her lead, and lo and behold, the bloodshed did come to an end. Bloodshed ended, peace reigned, and men began developing mutual trust after having been veritable wolves to one another. Blood ties mitigated their madness and they developed such familiarity that they no longer hesitated to conclude business deals with each other. Foreigners brought their families from neighboring islands, and even from kingdoms on distant shores. This was followed by allowing local tribesmen to marry their daughters, and before long her countrymen had begun embarking on voyages to distant islands and to kingdoms across the seas. The peoples continued to reap the fruits of peace born of the message of love until, one day, the horizon yielded the specter of a visitor from the farthest reaches of the East.

The new guest might have been tamed with embraces ever thirsty to acquire offspring had it not been for the interference of "the Book." Of course, the only reason this Book had become a pretext for enmity was its adherents' desperate appeal to its letter rather than its spirit. This was a development she had anticipated from the start even though she had learned from her contact with followers of other religions that all Scriptures are essentially a single revelation containing the commands of the one sovereign Lord. The only difference among Scriptures was that they were revealed in the various languages of the people who received them. All Scriptures were sent by the one Deity, whom the nations of the world have called by a variety of names. In the territories governed by the Seer of the Generation, the Deity had taken on the name of the Goddess Tanit, while among members of the Al Ibran tribe inhabiting Thouda, He had borrowed the name Elohim. Similarly, He was referred to as Dios by the inhabitants of Mallorca, and Allah by the horsemen of the new intruder.

As for the teachings of their various religions, Dahiya had long understood that the Scripture of the Hebrews, like that of the Europeans from beyond the sea, was in essence the same as her own ancient Scripture, known in the ancestors' tongue as Anhi. As she would learn later from her adopted son, the Arabs' Scripture was also no different in essence from those that had preceded it. All of these Scriptures were, simply put, the treasure she had lost in Anhi, and which the one Lord had willed to be rescued from oblivion.

There was also another lost prize that had been graciously restored to her: love. Thanks to love, she had been able to reunite the tribes of the homeland and establish the foundations of peace with tribes from elsewhere. If the winds of fortune blew her way and she was able to grasp both prizes in a single fist, she would have won the most priceless treasure of all. The question was: Would the wounded lion be persuaded by her argument and agree to worship with her in the Temple of Love—the one sanctuary capable of recovering the peace they had lost?

22

Martyrdom

THE CURSE OF THE LION was pride! His curse was pride even
when he was of sound body. How much more of a curse
would it be now that he was weakened with wounds? He
would repair to the first hidcout he came to, lick his wounds as
he waited to heal, and then, as always, go on a new offensive.
She couldn't help but chuckle when her spies informed her
that this Hassan, not content to lick the wounds of his defeat
in Barca, had engrossed himself in building projects there,
immortalizing his memory by erecting mansions after having
failed to immortalize it by the sword! It was also said that he
had stationed himself there on orders from his sovereign, who
occupied a throne somewhere in the distant regions of the
East, until reinforcements arrived from other nations that had
been subjugated by the Arabs.

This meant she would have to prepare to wage deadly war
not only against the Arabs, but against the entire East, if not
against the four corners of the earth, since the Arabs, as she was
told, had taken over all the kingdoms on Earth. The only ones
left standing in their path were the inhabitants of the unruly
backwater over which the Goddess had given her jurisdiction.
Still, she was capable of protecting them from bloodshed. She
could have protected the Arabs themselves from bloodshed
if they had placed their affairs in the hands of someone who
embraced the creed of love as she did, someone who appealed
not to the letter of the Scriptures, but to their spirit.

She did not believe, nor did she want to believe, that on their way to her, the invaders had lost sight of their Scripture's inward truth. However, the mean-spirited among the Arabs had robbed them of their true message and mission by exalting material gain as the purpose of their expeditions. As she had learned over the course of her life, this did not bode well, since disputes that arise over spoils are bound not only to grow intractable, but to deteriorate into out-and-out enmity.

Like all those who had gone before her, al-Kahina had sought to persuade the invaders to agree to spare people's lives in exchange for money, silver, and gold. However, they rejected such a truce as blasphemy against their Book, stipulating that in addition to the proposed "ransom," her people must embrace the Book's teachings and perform its prescribed rites. However, when some individuals such as Kusaila and the leader of the Garamantes had assented to the aggressors' demand in order to avoid bloodshed, they had soon been betrayed and subjected to all manner of abuse and humiliation: They had cut off the nose of the Garamantes' venerable leader on the pretext that he was plotting to wage war on the Arabs, and humiliated Kusaila by forcing him to skin sacrificial animals as his servants and followers looked on.

She too had sought to purchase peace with money, not because she feared war, but out of a desire for a peace based on the law of love to which she had reverently surrendered herself. What is the Divine, if not love? Could It possibly be worthy of worship unless love constituted Its innermost essence?

In making these overtures, she had been mindful of the need to accept the contents of the invaders' Book as her own religious creed, since she had learned that all Scriptures—be they those that had been lost and recovered, forgotten due to the passage of time, or newly revealed through visions— had been kneaded from a single lump of clay. However, they refused her gesture. They refused it because they knew that if their ruler received wealth from her as a gift freely offered, he would no longer need their services. If this happened, he would release them from their military duties and abandon them to starvation, since the only profession they had ever mastered was wielding a sword! Consequently, they preferred to risk their lives fighting rather than to meet their end without a reward. For those who view themselves as soldiers, starvation is not simply a way of dying, but a way of dying tainted with ignominy. As for death in battle, it is an act of heroism, and in the case of fighters dedicated to spreading the teachings of a revealed Scripture, death on the battlefield is always met with divine approval. It is a covenant sealed with the stamp of the gods. Therefore, in the view of peoples who take pride in bearing a sacred burden such as a revealed Scripture, death by the sword is a form of martyrdom; it is not evidence of death, but a testimony to life.

How, then, was one to change the thinking of someone who made a profession of killing in the belief that killing would guarantee him life not just once, but twice: first by winning him worldly plunder, and second by winning him the martyrdom which, according to the promise of the Scripture, would intercede on his behalf in the life of eternity?

23

The Seed

SOMEONE WHO HAD WAGERED ON love like al-Kahina could not depend on horsemen, chivalry, or men's physical strength. Instead, she relied on the majesty of love, which mediated the relationship with bodies that would not know what to do with themselves if love had not intervened to snatch the only treasure they concealed: the seed of progeny!

Progeny is indeed the basis for men's existence; without this they would be nothing but ghosts that burden the earth. What evidence is there for such a claim? The evidence is that they have no hesitations about justifying their presence on Earth with their lust for murder! The strangest thing of all is that they are not ashamed to refer to this despicable conduct as heroism! When the sages of the tribe installed her as custodian of the nation's affairs, she set about to pull this rug out from under their feet. To wit, she recruited into the army's ranks women who within a short time managed to outdo the fiercest claimants to equestrian mastery, accomplishing feats that exposed men's phony acts of heroism for the shams that they were.

If the ancients had truly thought well of men, they would not have promulgated a law that calls for a woman to be appointed guardian over the nation and its affairs. Indeed, they recognized their object of worship as female, certain that the creature who was destined to give birth to the world out of her belly was alone worthy to exercise sovereignty over the world of people. This was why she relied on the mysteries that slumbered in men's loins rather than on men themselves and why, when the passing of the days robbed her of the ability to produce the milk by which she could forge covenants of sonship with the offspring of foreign intruders, she drew on ruses she had inherited from the ancients. She was thus able to make the offspring of strangers into a son of her own who could be a brother to her two other sons from two different religions. They were now made from clay which had been kneaded together with the blood of a woman who had once seen herself in a dream suckling all races on Earth. Now, they were virtually brothers, and none would dare lift a hand against the others.

He had come to her on his own two feet, as though the Fate that had woven the fabric of prophecy had sent him to her as a reward for her passion for the love she had appointed as her arbiter. Fate had driven him to her with sword in hand. However, that same Fate had caused the sword to break. According to certain soothsayers, the sword sometimes wields even greater authority than the gods. The sword had broken, but he had not surrendered. Instead, he had gone on fighting, shielding himself from the enemy's thrusts with its broken handle. It was as though he were fighting to the death to answer the call of the Unknown, which had ordained to deliver him to the woman whose son he would become. He had viewed her as an enemy to whom he would give a taste of the bitterness of bereavement. However, as we know from the wisdom she had inherited from the precepts of the people's lost law, what we view as an evil omen often turns into a bearer of glad tidings, just as, at times, what we had thought to be a bearer of glad tidings reveals itself as an evil omen. Thus, when interpreting prophecies and visions, vigilance and caution are in order!

24

Murder

NIGHT . . . NIGHT HAD ALWAYS BEEN her oasis, the place where she spent time alone after the darkness had swallowed up all creatures, muffled all sounds, and emptied the world of everything but silence. Like the realm of dreams, silence was fertile ground for visions, the domain of apparitions. Since childhood, daytime had been an executioner that punished her with the lashes of hatred, so she had hated it in return. Nighttime, by contrast, had been her chosen friend, the one that rushed to her aid and consoled her in her affliction. The night alone could extinguish the burning embers of loathing in the heart of her stepmother, as it would blind both her and the wretched father who was helpless to intervene. The night that had been her source of succor yesterday was, today, her intimate companion. There alone could she interpret impenetrable mysteries. After all, it was night that had taught the world's peoples the arts of divination and brought them prophecies from the Realm of the Unknown.

Yes, night is a wise, albeit unnamed entity that weaves destinies behind a veil. Or rather, night itself is the veil, and its word, the final verdict. Night holds sway in the Realms of the Unseen. It alone utters the authoritative word in matters of destiny. This means that it keeps the horror—the truth—a secret, which is why the world's people have declared enmity against it.

She was peering up at the stars, speaking in private to her intimate companion, the night, when suddenly the old man burst into her retreat. As he usually did when interrupting one of her private nocturnal sessions, he claimed he hadn't been able to sleep.

He told her that sleep had declared enmity against him of late. He was suffering from old age, a fact he had never admitted and would never admit. She smiled, stifling words that had nearly escaped her lips.

What she didn't say was, "Someone who is about to turn one hundred can't complain about sleep's unfriendliness if it's simply a sign of old age!"

Catching the gleam in her eye beneath the starlight, he smiled and remarked, "The ancestors didn't call a man old unless he'd crossed the threshold of one hundred and ten, since only then would it be time for him to join the procession of his forebears. Besides, you mustn't forget that they've made an exception for people like me. Do you know what that is?"

She made no comment, a knowing smile settling across her lips. She knew what he was getting at, but she had no desire to stifle him by telling him so and ruining the spontaneous chitchat he had grown accustomed to whenever he walked in on her retreats. She knew he was approaching her about some matter that, in his view, was nothing short of momentous!

Continuing, he explained, "Only those who've had the good fortune to remain in their homelands are entitled to grow old. As for people like me who were denied that opportunity, we don't get to grow old until we've spent enough time in our homelands to enjoy the bliss we were deprived of in our earlier years."

He fell silent for a brief time. Then, noticing that she had been eyeing him in the starlight, he bowed his head and, tightening his grip on his cane, said softly, "People have yet to recover from the horror of what you did to them at Béjaïa, yet here you are preparing yourself to do something even worse."

After a pause, he cast her an ominous glance as though he were delivering a command drawn from the storehouse of the people's lost Scripture. *"Dagh talgha hund taydadgh ariqqum itasasatand amdal azzar*—regarding a matter like this, you would be best advised to consult the earth first."

She said nothing, but the night whispered between them for a time in the language of the Unknown.

Then she returned to a topic she thought she had consigned to oblivion. Defending herself, she said, "I only drove the people out of Béjaïa and leveled the city behind them because I had received news that they intended to receive Hassan's army and allow him to fortify himself there in his war against me."

Unconvinced, the old man replied, "What you did shows that your Intuition had betrayed you. Instead of winning over a community that was like family to you, you drove them into the enemy's embrace. They had been your supporters, but you turned them against you."

"Besides," he added, "what harm would it have done for Hassan to take refuge within the walls of the disaster-stricken Béjaïa? His entering the city would have been tantamount to falling into captivity. Its people were actually laying a trap for him, and offering him to you as spoils for the taking."

At last, shifting where she sat, she rolled up her sleeves to reveal her amulet-covered arms as though she were seeking assistance from the Unseen, which illumined the stars with knowledge of its will to provide her with the wisdom she lacked.

"I didn't order the destruction of Béjaïa for fear that it would become an enemy stronghold. I had it wiped out in punishment for treason. Not long ago, it was attacked by people from beyond the sea and, rather than resisting them, the city's inhabitants sheltered and protected them out of fear and hunger. In so doing, they betrayed the covenant between us. They allied themselves with an invading enemy. Hence, the punishment fits the crime, and I have no regrets over an action that I'm sure taught them a lesson!"

"Would it not be better," he asked, "to take a lesson from the example left by Kusaila? He concluded a truce with the people of Kairouan, who were themselves intruders who had come to the city with enemy invaders. But when Kusaila was approached by the Muslim commander Zuhayr ibn Qays al-Balawi during his stay in the city, he didn't order the city razed. Rather, he left the city out of compassion, to spare its people the horrors of a siege, and in fulfillment of the pact he'd made with them."

The old man paused to catch his breath. After giving her a long look, he asked incredulously, "So, after committing a sin against the people of the land, you now intend to commit a sin against the land itself?"

The night grimaced, addressing them both through a prolonged, tense silence. At last, she said, "I have given a great deal of thought to the Arabs. Like swarms of locusts, they have suddenly become a blight on the countries of the world. And from what I can see, they will never leave me in peace unless I sacrifice the thing that brings them pouring into our land and annihilating its inhabitants. The only basis I can see for this deadly greed of theirs is the triple allure of cities, gold, and pasturelands. This is why I have decided to bring ruin upon my own country so that the Arabs will despair of trying to make it their own and go back to where they came from, never to return."

Silence intervened between them once again.

As the night held its breath, listening intently, the old man said, "The action you intend might serve as a deterrent. What you have failed to take into consideration, however, is the Scripture that drives them to action!"

"*Attahlil*—the Scripture?" she asked, puzzled.

"That's right," he replied. "The secret always lies hidden deep within the Scriptures. Allow me to remind you that the people who invaded our land from beyond the seas also came on the pretext of spreading the message that lay within

112

their holy book. We have accounts from our ancestors telling how the tribes of Banu Ibran came claiming to propagate the content of their Scripture as well. Now people's homelands are facing something similar. As long as Scripture is what has brought them here, attempts to repel them by wiping entire cities off the face of the earth will do no good—indeed, it would be a stroke of madness—unless you were to pretend to believe the message contained in the Scripture."

Smiling disdainfully, she asked, "What use would there be in embracing the 'gospel' embedded in the folds of the Scripture they bring? Just look at the painful end Kusaila met after he did as much!"

Thereupon she proceeded to cite the sad stories of people who had believed in the new religion, but whose profession of faith had done nothing to protect them from having to pay the jizya. Worse still, when drought rendered them unable to pay the tax, their daughters were taken away from them to repay the debt!

In conclusion, she declared, "The purpose for their invasions has never been to lead the world's people to the sanctuary of the Deity, but simply to amass fleeting worldly gain that could most surely have been acquired without needing to commit murderous acts forbidden by their Deity—nay, acts condemned by all revealed Scriptures!"

After a pause, she added in a pained voice, "Something I've never been able to condone is murder. Indeed, I would be willing to sacrifice everything on Earth in offering to the Goddess Tanit if it would quench people's bloodlust!"

25

The Longest Stretch of Shade on Earth

SAGES RELATE THAT FROM TIME immemorial, this land had formed the longest stretch of Shade in the world—that is, until it was trampled beneath the hooves of Arab warriors' steeds. This mighty belt of Shade stretched from the frontiers of the timeless metropolis, Tripoli, to the outskirts of Tangiers in the distant West. A lush stretch imbued with the fragrance of rich soil, it was moist with the breaths of the sea which, remaining ever near, escorted it on its lengthy journey—nay, in its frenzied race—toward the West. Adept in the arts of seduction, this West never wearied of luring its seekers onward, waving the banners of intimate promise and enticing them with a dream, a treasure, or an extraordinary find that would embody deliverance somewhere beyond the horizon. It was this West that reigned supreme, and to which the nations flocked like the lost oasis of Waw of which the legends speak.

The Shade . . . sweeping doggedly onward, the stretch of Shade accompanied the sea along its tenacious path, in all its twists and turns, in its circumambulation around itself, in pursuit of the dream that makes its abode in the Unknown on some isthmus inhabiting the Lost Dimension.

This belt of Shade was filled with all manner of trees. Most of them were fruit bearing, a few were barren, but none begrudged gifts that had provided cures for a variety of ailments down the generations. Consequently, they were sought after by druggists and herbalists the world over, from the farthest reaches of the East and from lands beyond the seas.

Nevertheless, this precious strip of land would not have been viewed by the tribes as such a paradise had it not bordered the harshest, vastest, and most wickedly scorching desert of the known world. It stood erect along the desert's frontiers like a sentinel whom the Earth had commissioned to provide a refuge for its creatures down the generations, and to watch over the denizens of the nations. Thus, it had been sought out since time immemorial by peoples in search of deliverance from the ravages of thirst. Yet only those who had been cauterized by the desert flames could fathom the true importance of this legendary belt of Shade which, clothed in the seacoasts, traversed their forbidding expanse toward the destination that the nations have ever and always vied to reach, and in whose sanctuary they have striven to pray: the West!

Although the Shade liberally bestowed safe haven from the fire, it did not content itself solely with its identity as Shade. For those who had migrated from the scorching desert to this blessed refuge were generally not satisfied with the mere existence of the Shade, but went on to make fruitful use of the abundance of water thanks to which the Shade had come to be. To wit, they cultivated the soil, thereby infusing their presence with meaning and consecrating their residence in the Shade's priceless expanse. In so doing, they left the fingerprint of a frenzied preoccupation born of fear and dread as they sought to impart meaning to their quest. This purpose would never be complete, of course, without constructing a place of worship in which to lift prayers of gratitude to the Deity that had protected them from thirst and bestowed upon them the blessed Shade.

Their regular circuits around the sacred precinct led them eventually to build other structures to provide shelter from the seasonal rains and wild storms that the Mother of All Deserts exhaled mercilessly onto the Shade. The migrants from the fiery desert also constructed buildings as a way of seeking blessing from the tombs they had erected in honor of revered souls whose spirits had passed on. Hence, they referred to these structures not as repositories of the dead but, rather, as dwellings of the living. Before long, such monuments to civilization—some of them of clay and others of stone—had grown in size and number until they took the form of impregnable fortresses planted along the Shade's lengthy path, which extended valiantly onward toward the hoped-for refuge that lay nestled in some hidden part of an ever-missing dimension to which the nations of the world referred cryptically as "the West."

With the passing of the days and years, urban life in the Kingdom of the Shade continued to evolve, giving birth to growing numbers of family lines. Priding itself on its fortunes, it became an abode of proverbial opulence and luxury. It thus drew strangers from all parts, who flocked to it in search of affluence, and who established covenants with the Kingdom of the Shade in the form of commercial agreements. Still other nations flocked there in search of protection and chose to make it their home. Before long, such settlers began to reproduce, ethnicities intermingled, and they multiplied and multiplied—all thanks to the Shade.

This was the Shade that the Priestess of the Generations had decided to eradicate. She ordered her men to cut down its trees and raze its fortresses, destroying every remnant of civilization and vegetation alike. She did so in the belief that wiping the Shade off the face of the earth and joining the moist soil of the north with its arid counterpart in the south would shield her from the Arabs, who had only come out against her out of greed for a civilization they had forfeited in their own homelands. It is said that when the elders of the nation pleaded with her to rescind her verdict, she declared without hesitation that the only way to guard against the Arab hordes' thirst for booty would be to strip the coasts of their inviting canopy and cause

117

the place to revert to its original fiery state: bare of shade, and washed clean by the blessed spring of freedom.

As for the bard of Thouda, who shadowed the Seer wherever he went, he extolled the eradication in verse, saying: "The Shade is the word of the night against the day, while its eradication is the day's argument against the night!"

26

The Obliteration

OVER THE WEEKS THAT FOLLOWED, the old man hovered about her, repeating his insistence that she consult the earth concerning her intentions. It was as though the lost law were disguised within his feeble frame. When at last his strength gave out, he appealed to a teaching which he said was taken from the Old Scripture:

Awakanan wayyazzaranin dagh watyan
Ittakhalun wayyaharinin dagh hilan.
What the ancestors built over generations
Is wiped out by their successors in a matter of nights.

He went about repeating this dictum for days on end. Then, it is said, he attempted to persuade the bard of Thouda to allow him to teach it to him so that he could circulate it among the people in his melodious voice. However, obsessed with the mournful songs he composed with such mastery to instill fervor in young soldiers' hearts for the anticipated battle, the poet disappointed the venerable elder.

Crestfallen, the poor man retreated to his tent to fight off the blazing fever. Made from the skins of wild animals, the tent had been erected for him in the Priestess's new camp along the path of her eastward advance in search of the wounded lion. She was determined to make herself such a nightmare to him that he would find no peace in his most recent hideaway.

Before long, she went and knocked on her elder's tent door bearing the panacea, as she referred to it. She explained that she had only come to heal him of his dread disease, of the malady that had afflicted him since he was driven out of his beloved desert on account of family ties for which he bore no responsibility. According to a custom decreed by law, tribal leaders could only be succeeded by their maternal nephews; the right of succession was denied even to their own sons. By a twist of fate, he had been forced to pay the price for this custom by being exiled from his homeland for decades, since the tribal leaders' sons, thirsty for power, would have been unable to rule as long as he—the leader's sole maternal nephew—was among them. He had been left with no choice but to flee into exile.

Having come to deliver what she termed good news, al-Kahina told him that she had only ordered the destruction of the Kingdom of Shade in order to fulfill his age-old dream of appearing in the sanctuary of his beloved desert. She said, "Year after year, despite your repeated attempts, you have never been able to return to the forbidding expanses of your old Deity. So I have decided to outwit Fate by bringing the desert to you! Now at long last, the desert will seek *you* out!"

Continuing, she said, "Once my campaign of obliteration has been completed, the desert will advance against the arrogant North that has taken refuge in nearness to the vast sea. Gone will be the concentrations of edifices in whose shadows dead people slumber, thinking themselves alive. Such concentrations they refer to euphemistically as 'cities,' when in fact they would more accurately be described as cemeteries!"

When he said nothing in reply, she added, "I can take pride in the fact that I have delivered my people from slavery. I've freed them from confinement in crypts that they mistakenly believed to be homes simply because they offered protection from the heat and cold. The people had disregarded the fact that when they sought refuge in caves they had built with their own hands and concealed themselves from a sky washed clean with the light of eternal suns never veiled even by the clouds, they were betraying their covenant with the desert and selling their freedom for a pittance."

Drawing her impassioned defense to a close at last, she said, "You should be grateful to me for having realized how to restore your lost desert to you, allowing you once again to sleep peacefully in its arms as your ancestors once did rather than having to go in search of ways back to its impenetrable sanctuary. It would have been impossible to return there anyway, not only because of your advanced age, but because of the illusions of the time now past, illusions that rendered your return a crippling fixation and transformed your maternal cousins into phantoms that lay in wait for you with knives, even in your sleep!"

27

The Abode

AL-KAHINA'S ENCOUNTER WITH HER AGING guardian would prove to be far easier than that with the tribal elders. Following a time of continual strife, with blades sinking into flesh and growing bloodshed, the leaders of the tribes had no choice but to exchange messengers. After forming delegations from various regions in the lush belt of Shade, they approached the Majestic Seer in hopes of presenting an argument that would persuade her to relinquish her pride and relieve their affliction.

Delegations flocked to her place of retreat, on their lips a burning question to which they either had found no answer, or an answer which had left them more puzzled and agitated than the question itself. The message bearers sent out to their regions on horseback had said, "In order to force the invaders to turn back, we have no choice but to confront them with another desert. Only then will they despair and retreat to their own wasteland." However, this argument had not persuaded them, as they were certain that obliterating the Belt of Shade and bringing their homes down on their heads would do nothing to protect them from the swords of the invaders. On the contrary, now that the invaders knew the truth about the abundance they enjoyed, and had tasted the delectable fruits of their land, they would never leave them in peace!

As was her custom, the Seer received them with the honorific ceremonies that befit their station. Animals were slaughtered in their honor, and skilled horsemen presented them with displays of their equestrian martial arts. Before opening serious debate, she summoned the bard from Thouda to laud their ancestors' heroic feats in melodious verse.

"Of what benefit is it," she asked, "to build structures to live in, whether of brick or stone, if they fail to protect us from the brute force of an aggressor who can besiege us from all sides and drive us to hunger and thirst, then exterminate us like so many rats? Do you not see that those who seek protection within walls have chosen to be confined not under duress, but of their own free will? Whenever you come under attack by the alien nations that are vomited up by the malicious sea, it is your powerful, free desert comrades who come to liberate you from your self-made prisons in the Land of the Shade."

The Seer fell silent for a time, pausing to gauge the impact of her words. She then went on to state the conclusion she had reached concerning the true character of those who had chosen the Shade as their abode and refuge, only to find themselves unable to defend what they held most sacred. After all, a fortress isn't a home but, rather, a stronghold where prisoners languish as they await a fate to be decided by the most cowardly adventurer ever to unsheathe a sword. In short, those who had sought out the Shade had made voluntary hostages of themselves.

She scowled so fiercely that sparks gleamed in her eyes, which were still as piercing as ever despite the years she had spent battling the ghosts of the Realms of the Unseen. Then she uttered an epithet viewed as so offensive among the peoples of the day that it was a source of ignominy—nay, a curse. As if she were spitting the word out, so great was her contempt, she fumed, "*Awin ikalan wajjigh mayddan!* These aren't men—they're nothing but slaves!"

The place was convulsed with an uproar as bewildered queries mingled with cries of condemnation. However, the woman who had been accustomed to treating her wounds with tongues of fire rather than with ointments and medicinal herbs had no sympathy for people who, to her disgust, were content to spend their days lolling in houses of clay and whose affinity for life in the Shade had extinguished the flames of heroism in their hearts.

Incredulous, she asked, "Are you no longer ashamed to be taken by surprise by the most cowardly of cowards simply because he had the courage to unsheathe a sword and tear you out of your wives' arms before seizing the women and binding you in shackles of iron?"

As the assembly broke anew into an uproarious din, she added, "This is what happens every time your comrades in the desert fail to come to your rescue. Something you should know, and which the tribes have learned down the years from experience and the ancient commands, is that whoever longs for deliverance has only to cling to the desert for refuge. Never has the desert forsaken anyone who sought safety there from affliction. Those who have had the courage to choose the desert as their abode are invincible, since they alone bear their homes on their backs and hide their spoils in their hearts. Those who have been liberated from attachment to fleeting earthly treasures will be forever victorious. As for those who are content to live behind walls, they have chosen to defeat themselves before being defeated by any foe!"

After catching her breath, she appealed to the lost Scripture, from whose treasure she drew the truth that states, "*Nanai iliyalli yasidarfanan akli, bashshan waranni akli yasidarfanan iliyalli!* We have seen a free man liberate a slave, but never have we seen a slave liberate a free man!"

28

The Bridge
Barca, AH 81/703 CE

THE MAN ON WHOM THE custodians of the new Scripture were
relying to propagate its message by the sword in the unknown
regions of the West—the West inhabited by riddles, treasures,
and houris—stationed himself in a legendary place known in
the forgotten tongue of its original inhabitants as Barca.

Barca itself had been haunted by riddles and myths since
the days of old, when it was inhabited by the people from
beyond the seas. They had settled there after fleeing overpop-
ulated, war-torn homelands that had expelled the adherents
of religions enamored with the search for Truth. Long before
this, the coasts of Libya had received fierce folk from the
Roman Sea, who had come not to dwell there, but rather to
use it as a land bridge or crossroads between East and West.
It thus became an isthmus connecting two worlds, two mythic
dreams which, though distant from one another, had been
eternally thirsty to meet and fuse. Later, newcomers from the
land of Greece established the city of Barca, from which one
could set out eastward to explore the riddle of riddles known
as Misr—Egypt—or westward to seek out another, equally
legendary entity—Carthage, and the lands beyond.

Were East and West the only two sought-after destinations? By no means! Barca was also located along a road
that bridged two other destinations, each of which saw the
other as a mystery shrouded in legend. Barca pointed to the
unnamed, mysterious South, home to the fiercest peoples of

the old world: women who would marry dogs, tribes that fed on human flesh, or ghosts that bartered gold dust for its weight in grains of salt.

The fate of a place that served as a bridge was always an uncertain one. On the one hand, it was bound to be transformed into a commercial center because it was the point where various nations met to exchange goods of mutual benefit. On the other hand, there was no guarantee that this blessing would not become a curse if war broke out among these same nations. The locations most liable to be harmed by warring parties were those that served as bridges, and Barca had paid dearly over the centuries for its central position. Despite the prosperity it had enjoyed under Greek rule thanks to its role as a crossroads, it also suffered bitterly for this very reason when war broke out with the people of ancient Egypt to the East. Its woes then resumed for hundreds of years when the flames of war were ignited with Carthage to the West. Now it found itself reliving its ancient fate as it was trampled underfoot simultaneously by two armies: an army from the East in its perpetual advance on the West, and its own warriors as they resisted the invaders in repeated campaigns of attack and retreat.

29

Glory

AFTER HIS DEFEAT AT THE hands of the fearsome Seer, Hassan ibn al-Nu'man remained for five years in this time-honored strategic spot, adorned with the lofty edifices of bygone nations, to wait for reinforcements from the caliph ensconced in Damascus. If the reinforcements were delayed, he would return home by way of Egypt after the manner of the Muslim commanders who had preceded him in these parts. In fact, the reinforcements were delayed due to the sordid traps which the Umayyads were constantly setting for each other, and to which the innocent always fell prey.

Abd al-Aziz ibn Marwan, governor of Egypt and brother of the Caliph Abd al-Malik, had been authorized to appoint governors over the rest of the North in Egypt's capacity as the portal to the African continent. He had woven a conspiracy to hinder the arrival of the reinforcements needed by Ibn al-Nu'man. Given his unquenchable thirst for spoils, Abd al-Aziz envied Ibn al-Nu'man for his governorship over North Africa as no one else did. Not content to seize what he had no right to, he made repeated attempts to block even his brother's share of the spoils—without the latter's knowledge, of course. Located as he was halfway between North Africa and Damascus, he could engage in blatant thievery that would have ill befit even a highway robber, let alone the brother of the caliph!

Like a lion who had suffered a blow for which he had not been prepared, Ibn al-Nu'man had originally intended to station himself in Barca just long enough to regroup. When the wait dragged on, however, he often thought of fleeing to the Hijaz. In the meantime, he occupied himself with building projects as a diversion and pastime.

Ibn al-Nu'man was captivated by the idea of imitating earlier civilizations whose rich remains he had found still standing in Barca as though their builders had departed only days before. These imposing edifices included enchanting palaces, enormous marble pillars, and splendorous temples embellished with rich mosaics. So meticulously were they arranged and so generously adorned, it was as though the stones with which they were inlaid had been set in place not by human hands, but by elves and fairies.

Ibn al-Nu'man would constantly make the rounds of its buildings and wander through its theaters, which had been chiseled out of the foothills' diamond-hard boulders as though they had been brought straight down from the heavens by some legendary force rather than having been constructed by beings of flesh and blood. Their majestic, exquisite interiors seemed to have been divinely shielded from the slightest error of structure or execution, however incidental. Indeed, that which had been rendered exempt from the sin of an earth inhabited by creatures made up entirely of sin richly deserved to be flawless.

However, this very inviolability appears to have been what wiped out the place's inhabitants. The imposing structure towered above the forbidding mountain peak with a pride that befit a creation of the gods, beyond the reach of merely human religions, and looked out over a sea that was unashamed to kiss the flank of a mountain cut from an unnamed stone. From below it resembled a temple carved by the will of Mother Nature, which the Realms of the Unseen had topped with still another temple dedicated to the Lord of Lords, whose praises had been sung by the priests of nations now long gone.

The radiant, if dimming, glory of what remained had prompted Ibn al-Nu'man to imitate the genius of the peoples who had gone before. He realized that the glory achieved by towering monuments is the most tawdry of all. However, defeat had taught him that a glory etched in stone is better than no glory at all. He had suffered the sting of a humiliating defeat at the hands of a woman (even if she was no ordinary woman), and had no choice but to try his luck at building, even if his purpose in doing so was mere diversion. Any action, however lowly, would be preferable to waiting passively at the mercy of the Umayyads, whose machinations and internecine squabbles had brought disaster on their supporters time and time again. Never had they elevated anyone in order to bestow honor, but only to humiliate. They would favor those who had given their allegiance and support until they had served their purpose, after which they would spit them out and grind them into the dust!

Ibn al-Nu'man knew that a glory which had not been achieved with the swords of heroism was no glory at all, but only a shadow thereof. What sort of glory could be achieved under the rule of an invidious monarch like Abd al-Malik ibn Marwan or a rancorous governor like his brother Abd al-Aziz? Never once had he appeased either of them with beautiful slave women or loads of money but that the other had seethed with resentment. It was as though they were contemptible rivals constantly scheming against each other, not partners in the exercise of authority, still less blood brothers. All he could see in these two pitiful creatures was a couple of impudent little boys or catty co-wives who couldn't bear each other's company and wouldn't rest until they had committed the most abhorrent offenses against each other. He found it so repugnant to be associated with them that he envied Hanash Sanaani for having joined Ibn al-Zubayr's gang. He saw clearly now that it was impossible to please a tyrant, no matter how pious, and no matter how earnestly said tyrant might pretend to be seeking divine approval.

Divine approval? Divine approval had been his dream, nay, his daily obsession, and never once had he imagined that the likes of Abd al-Malik ibn Marwan or his brother Abd al-Aziz would come along and rob him of this aspiration. He had once seen their appointment of him as governor over North Africa as a golden opportunity to achieve his dream of opening polytheists' hearts and ushering them into God's religion in droves. Yet he had found himself among people for whom divine approval had never once been of the least concern. On the contrary, their sole aim was to amass spoils or snag the largest number of slave women. In so doing, of course, they had bartered away the spoils of the life to come in return for those of the ephemeral realm. He had heard it whispered here and there that he had not been left in limbo all those years because of his defeat at the hands of a trickster of a woman but rather, because of his failure to properly divide the spoils of war between the two feuding brothers.

Ibn al-Nu'man had been at a loss as to how to resolve this dilemma. Whenever he showered the caliph with spoils in his capacity as Commander of the Faithful, he was certain to earn the wrath of Abd al-Aziz, perched on his throne in Egypt, in double measure. Abd al-Aziz considered himself most worthy of the lion's share since he, not Abd al-Malik—who lived immersed in opulence in remote Damascus—had appointed Ibn al-Nu'man governor over North Africa, which meant that he, not the caliph, was Ibn al-Nu'man's true benefactor.

If, on the other hand, Ibn al-Nu'man did the opposite and set aside a satisfactory share for Abd al-Aziz as he passed through Egypt, Abd al-Malik would fly into a rage, furious with him for daring to divide his gifts equally with Abd al-Aziz, whose status as his brother counted for nothing in his eyes. On the contrary, as far as Abd al-Malik was concerned, his brother was nothing but a ne'er-do-well who didn't deserve his appointment as governor over a timeless beacon like Egypt!

Ibn al-Nu'man retreated into seclusion and after long thought, concluded that the only way to escape this nightmarish conflict would be to seek refuge in his building enterprise, however short-lived it might be, in the hope that it would shield him from the harm that might otherwise befall him on account of the brothers' rivalry. If his construction endeavors failed to perform this function, he would lose little, since raising walls was the one feat the Umayyads were unlikely to envy him for!

30

The Obstacle

IN THE END, IBN AL-NU'MAN's only recourse in the face of his calamity was to go on building.

His calamity? Was it just one calamity? In fact, there had been two. The first had been his failure to please God because he had been defeated before the enemy of God, and the second was his failure to appease those whom God had appointed in His Book as vicegerents of His Majesty on Earth. He had discovered how difficult it was to please his fellow man, particularly if the fellow man happened to be someone with authority over him, and most especially a ruler with the power to decide whether he lived or died. If he had the further misfortune of falling victim to two wills in conflict—two rulers at loggerheads—this would be the most unenviable fate of all, even if he appeared to be the fortunate possessor of power over everything that crept on the face of the earth or hid within its depths.

Be that as it may, he buried his distress in the process of building proud monuments which came to be known by the illustrious epithet "Hassan's palaces," as though, in keeping with the divine teaching that God will never withhold reward from someone who has done a job well, Fate had insisted on giving credit where credit was due.

Ibn al-Nu'man confided his despair to his assistants and to the notables of Quraysh who had accompanied him on the expedition but who, after being taken captive, had been ordered released by the majestic Seer. (Thanks to this magnanimous gesture, they boasted that God had granted them a second birth of sorts, although, in reality, it was now a debt that hung around their necks.) He told them that even if he received the most abundant reinforcements in the world, he no longer intended to pursue a campaign that had not truly been launched for the sake of God, and that if given the choice, he would relinquish his post and return to the East as so many others had done. This gesture gained Ibn al-Nu'man added favor in the eyes of his supporters, who responded with a sympathy and gratitude that snuffed out the envy some of them had felt. In fact, his erstwhile opponents were won over to his side.

Of course, Ibn al-Nu'man's inclination to abandon his military expedition did not mean surrender. On the contrary, he continued to gather information about his enemy on the other side of the bridge. Spies would bring him reports on her comings and goings, her intentions, and her last readings of the tablet from the Realm of the Unseen. He marveled at the cunning and intelligence which had enabled her to overlook personal whim and preference and, demonstrating tolerance and foresight, release scores of notables she had taken captive and even adopt an enemy soldier as her own son. Recognizing her wisdom, he felt certain that were he able to persuade this woman to relinquish her pride and embrace Islam, he would earn the abundant approval of the Most Merciful.

Uqba ibn Nafi's aggression against the great leader Kusaila had become a stumbling block that prevented other leading figures in North Africa from embracing Islam. It had descended as a curse upon the mission to spread the religion. The heady victories achieved by Muslim commanders had led them astray and the lust for spoils had extinguished the flame of true guidance in their souls. As a consequence, they had allowed themselves to engage in actions which, in the eyes of the vanquished, bespoke a tyranny no different from that of any other invader. This ill-fated incident (for which Ibn Nafi had paid with his life, and for which the religion of Truth had paid more dearly still) delayed the spread of the Islamic message by decades. As for the believers, the price they paid was precious blood spilled and honorable lives lost. These were sacrifices they would not have had to make had they clung to "the most trustworthy hand-hold"[7] spoken of in their Scripture, and had they put to death the demons of selfish desire and infatuation with violent conflict as they had been taught to do by the imams of the pure religion.

31

The Lifeline

As the Seer was celebrating the sight of stones tumbling and trees being felled at her followers' hands, Ibn al-Nu'man, whom she never tired of dubbing *al-jarih* ("the wounded"), received the bizarre news of the step she had undertaken. When he first learned of the matter, he was shaken to the core. However, it was not long before he saw in it a glad tiding from heaven itself, a free gift from the hand of the Almighty which he was determined to put to the best possible use.

Happily, his intuition proved correct, for not long thereafter he began receiving delegations from the tribes, which had come to him appealing for help in the wake of the horror that had befallen them, and asking that he do whatever he could to protect them from the madness of a woman who had finally lost her senses.

When he was alone, he often wondered about the idolatry that maims people's souls, causing them to reject a faith that is a natural part of them and sell their salvation for a pittance— the pittance of error—all on account of an overweening, false pride and blind trust in impulses whose proneness to evil everyone knows from bitter experience. Otherwise, what harm would it have done her to wash her heart clean with faith? What harm would it have done her to forgive enemy commanders who were fallible human beings just as she was, recognizing that even though they were heralds sent forth to spread a message, they were still subject to the allure of sin and caprice? How much better she could have protected herself and her people from the horrors of combat if she had only demonstrated some tolerance!

He recognized the sins his forebears had committed against the people, from Abdullah ibn Abi Sarh to Qays al-Balawi, and Uqba before him, of course. But as the nations of the world had experienced since time immemorial, the punishments for the sins of earlier generations are suffered by the generations that succeed them. Since the time he had set foot in these lands, he had been paying the price for his predecessors' sins in successive installments, the cruelest of which had been the recent humiliating defeat that had nearly cost him his life.

What is a believer's life, if not a postponed ransom awaiting the day when it will obtain the hoped-for salvation of martyrdom?

True loss is not death for God's sake but, rather, failure to fulfill one's duty, that is, losing the battle. Losing a battle might be forgivable if the battle concerned had not been waged in order to exalt the word of God and demonstrate surrender to the divine will. In such a case, martyrdom is deliverance. He could not have borne remaining alive after that agonizing defeat had it not been for his certainty that surviving was his only hope of repeating the attempt which, even if it was not crowned with the exaltation of God's word, would be crowned, at the very least, with the martyrdom of someone who had loved God and who saw in his meeting of God a lifeline to salvation.

32

Money

THE IDEA SPRANG INTO CONSCIOUSNESS as if by revelation: Khalid ibn Yazid! Throughout the time he had spent searching for ways to resume his military campaign, Ibn al-Nu'man had forgotten that he had a resident spy in Her Majesty's court, and that all he had to do was send a messenger inquiring of him about her affairs and conditions in her alleged realm. This would not be an act of espionage, as some might foolishly think, but rather a prudent attempt to test out the waters, to explore the state of play, and to locate potential traps and threats. If the attempt yielded the desired information, it might enable him to develop a plan that would spare him the need to wait for reinforcements. After all, many a mighty army has tasted the bitterness of defeat at the hands of a contemptible foe simply because its leaders made light of the opposition's strengths and resources, and because they failed to properly inform themselves of the facts on the ground.

He jumped to his feet, ready to go inspect his building projects as he did whenever he was weighed down by melancholy, his chest tight with the distress that had become his daily fare. This time, however, he set out energized by the headiness of the glad tidings he had received. Without realizing what he was doing, he even began humming a sentimental tune. The moment he became aware of himself, he cursed Satan, his tongue waxing prolix in pleas for forgiveness!

Once he had composed himself, he instructed the guard patrols to summon the scout without delay. He lingered atop a boulder to contemplate his work, which he now saw in the light of a heart aglow with inspiration. What he saw was good—more than good, it was worthy of becoming a relic durable enough to challenge the tyrant of tyrants, Time itself. It was not stones that he relied upon in his duel to bring down Time's cunning and arrogance but, rather, the message to be etched in those stones.

Once the patrol had brought the scout, Ibn al-Nu'man prepared to dictate a message to Khalid ibn Yazid. As he was about to do so, however, he thought better of it, and instead ordered a parchment and an inkwell be brought to him. He preferred to draft a letter, not because the written word grants the content some sacred value simply by virtue of its being guarded by seals, but rather because he feared that the message might be compromised by the curiosity of common folk. A scout isn't some angel above foolish talk or blunders who can be fully depended upon in relation to such a weighty matter. On the contrary, he is a mere courier who at the first rest stop he comes to will blurt out whatever message he's been entrusted with to passersby who are themselves either scouts or spies. He therefore chose to send his message in written form in order to receive a written missive in response. This would be far better than receiving a spoken version on the lips of the messenger, who could be heard by one and all as though he had been sent not to preserve a trust, but to broadcast the news to everyone near and far.

Ibn al-Nu'man composed his missive in the open space that surrounded the edifices he had constructed, some distance away from the army's camp site. Thanks to the army's long stay in the area since he first ordered it to encamp there when fleeing the ghost of his miserable defeat, not to mention the abundance of trade caravans that continuously intersected there, the site had developed into a bustling population center with markets in the middle of the settlements.

After dismissing the messenger and excusing himself from the patrol, Ibn al-Nu'man made his way westward until he reached a hill turbaned in pine trees where he retreated whenever he was dogged by melancholy and angst. While there, he wrestled with another concern still more burdensome than awaiting reports on the conditions of the Priestess: the need for reinforcements. Without them, he could not risk going into battle with his remaining soldiers, for whom he bore a responsibility not only before the caliph—or the caliph of the caliph entrenched in Fustat—but even more importantly, before God.

What he had not yet been able to decide was which of the two caliphs to approach with the matter. Should he go to Abd al-Malik ibn Marwan, Commander of the Faithful, or the person whom the Commander of the Faithful had placed in authority over him—Abd al-Aziz ibn Marwan, Governor of Egypt? He had faced difficulties from the very start of his tenure in North Africa because these two brothers' powers over the region overlapped in a way unparalleled by any other of the scattered regions under the caliphate's rule.

Who, he wondered, had established the foolish tradition of treating the Governor of Egypt as the guardian over the entire continent of Africa simply because it was the portal to this vast labyrinth? Did it date back to the era of Uthman ibn Affan? It would certainly have been in character for Ibn Affan to introduce such a policy. Uthman ibn Affan was the instigator of all the transgressions ever committed against the various metropolises by the Caliphal State, not least of which was the installation in Egypt of Abdullah ibn Abi Sarh—an apostate against whom the Apostle himself had declared open season for his blasphemy. Abdullah ibn Abi Sarh had been appointed guardian over North Africa simply because he was Ibn Affan's milk brother. He was portrayed as a proponent of a religion he had never believed in. Moreover, the choice of this devotee of material gain as guardian over the religion had sparked civil and religious unrest that caused bloodshed in the Muslim community from that day onward.

One thing certain was that he was bound to suffer harm regardless of which of the two men he addressed. If he approached Abd al-Aziz, he would actually be dealing with a middleman who would bring the matter to the caliph. Being a mere connecting link between Ibn al-Nu'man and the caliph, Abd al-Aziz would be powerless to do anything of his own accord even if it concerned only himself. How much less power would he have, then, to dispose of an entire army which only the caliph possessed the authority to mobilize? Besides, by approaching Abd al-Aziz, he would risk wounding the pride of the caliph in his capacity not only as leader of the Muslims, but as God's vicegerent on Earth.

If Ibn al-Nu'man mustered the boldness to approach the caliph himself, he might earn the caliph's gratitude. However, he would most certainly forfeit the approval of Abd al-Aziz. But . . . why should he fear the wrath of Abd al-Aziz ibn Marwan? Whence had the state's coffers been filled throughout the years past if not from the treasures of North Africa? Why should he fear the indignation of a ruler who was himself ruled by another, and whose superior would dismiss him without hesitation if he dared conceal from him his share of the spoils or money? Wasn't money the ruler of the world that could threaten the well-being of the caliph himself if the state exchequer were emptied?

Wasn't the caliph, and the caliph alone, worthy to issue commands and prohibitions? If so, then why should he abase himself before the likes of Abd al-Aziz ibn Marwan, or the House of Marwan, or even the entire tribe of Banu Umayya? God knows they had never boasted a single virtue that would have rendered them worthy to rule. Indeed, they would never have come to power if the Fates hadn't rushed to their aid. The Fates, of course, bestow their generosity not to honor people, but to put them to the test!

Given the blessed tidings that had descended upon him thanks to the blunder the Seer had committed at her people's expense, Ibn al-Nu'man felt confident that those in authority would respond to his plea.

33

Freedom

On his way to see the tool of intrigue whom the Fates had slipped unawares into the Genie's sleeve, the messenger sought to come up with a ruse that would enable him to achieve his aim—but all he found was hope!

It has been said that prostitution is the only ruse by which women can get what they need, while men are at a loss for ways to do the same. As for the peoples of the world, the only way they have found to obtain a share of their own is to beg. They have contented themselves with this ruse, despite the humiliation it entails, consoled by the fact that such humiliation pales beside that endured by women forced to prostitute themselves.

The messenger turned his horse aside onto a foothill ringed with pine trees, then emerged from a thicket after donning someone else's skin. Leaving his mount and his belongings in a cave hidden along the side of the mountain, he descended along its western flank. At length he came upon a scattering of huts belonging to peasants engaged in a noble struggle to wrest their daily sustenance from the grip of a stern Mother who refuses to yield her gifts without sacrifice and toil.

He headed toward the elevated spot where he had come on an earlier occasion. When he had come the first time, he had done so as the messenger of a mighty leader on whose behalf he had spoken from a position of strength. At that time, he had represented a party with the power to impose its will. This time he had come in secret, disguised as a beggar clothed in rags of ignominy!

Before arriving, he remembered to sprinkle his face and hair with dirt. Not content with this disguise, he painted his features with a look of misery and his eyes with sorrow. He had entertained the wicked idea of faking a physical handicap, such as a limp or blindness in one eye, thereby adding to the impression of helplessness. But he ruled out the idea for fear that it might bring ill fortune.

In the orchards enclosed within the walls of the fortress where the Priestess made her home, he kept watch for the man he had come to see. With hunched back and dejected mien, he hovered about the place, muddied hand stretched forth. However, the man was nowhere to be seen. When the sun began to set, he had yet to appear. Hence, the messenger-turned-mendicant was forced to spend the night in the woods nearby, cushioning his head on his arm and praising God for the clement weather, since otherwise he would have perished from the cold in those unforgiving parts.

Even so, the messenger had to admit to himself that the entire time he was engaged in this childish game, he had experienced a subtle, covert enjoyment. He wondered whether this feeling was what Muslim divines had described as "happiness." Happiness? The astute imams of the faith had spoken of this griffon in such veiled language that it had been rendered an impenetrable enigma. Could happiness possibly be so within reach? And if so, what right did he have to it? By virtue of what heroic feat had he merited such a prize? Might this be the reason for his childlike urge to wiggle out of a costume which, by force of habit, had become second-nature to him? Even though it set him apart and was acknowledged by others as "his," it had never reflected who he really was.

Was this persona that had been willed upon him by others simply a contrived entity that he had had no part in creating? Had he simply put it on like the many borrowed garments in which he strutted proudly about, not because they were comfortable, but because they impressed onlookers?

Was this why coarse woolen garments had so appealed to the likes of Hanash Sanaani, Abu Dharr al-Ghifari, and all the dervishes who had embraced asceticism alongside their professed creed? Was it really possible that simply disguising oneself in the tattered rags of a beggar could achieve a happiness that religious teachers had held up as an impossible ideal? Perhaps this kind of disguise was a return to a pristine state that he had lost by panting after others' approval instead of embracing what met with his own. And perhaps this state had freed him from a burden that was heavier than he had ever realized. The happiness that religious scholars had expounded on with a prolixity that had once left him with a headache turned out—like freedom—to be closer to him than his jugular vein.

34

The Loaf of Bread

HIS BLISSFUL STATE LINGERED THROUGH the following day, and
the day after, when at last he captured his prey. When he found
himself in Ibn Yazid's presence that day, he stood there calmly,
as though he hadn't truly wanted to overtake him, so delighted
was he with the serendipitous find he had made thanks to his
childish caper! As he stammered the password, Ibn Yazid's
features brightened. He then placed some alms in the messenger qua beggar's outstretched hand, whereupon he hurriedly
gave him the scroll with a knowing gesture.

Ibn Yazid scrutinized the scroll for a few moments before
murmuring hastily, "Give me till tomorrow, and I shall have
an answer for you." Then he turned and rushed off in a mud-
dle that ill-befit the station of a queen's son, even if he was
only a son by adoption!

The messenger watched Ibn Yazid until he had disappeared
from sight and imagined him poring over the parchment.

After reading the message, Ibn Yazid requested a quill
and prepared to pen on the back of the parchment the reply
that would bring about the demise of his rescuer and benefactor—nay, his milk mother, as he was destined to learn later.
Somewhere within him there stirred a vague ache which, after
some reflection, he recognized as what the virtuous generally
refer to as "conscience."

Later that evening—not the following day as he had promised—he surprised the messenger with a loaf of sand-baked

bread inside of which, he told him, he would find his answer to the missive from Ibn al-Nu'man. Then, with a wave of the hand, he bade him farewell.

Hardly had the messenger set out toward his lair in the mountainous heights than his being was rent asunder by a dreadful, throaty screech that would have raised the dead from their graves. Before long, such a violent clamor arose in response to the horrific shriek that the mountain itself seemed to be going to pieces. Women's wails, men's shouts, and children's screams mingled with the thunder of horsemen racing in all directions in response to a summons from the Unknown—a resounding summons issued in the tongue of Realms Unseen. The voices heard that day would be conveyed to later generations in the annals of history, penned by those with a passion to preserve its events, and summed up in the words:

Ikallan nun ijalan dagh awatattan middan nawan!
Your rule has been lost to a mere morsel of bread!

Shaken to the core as the contagion of fear spread, he took off running, only to realize that the alarm being sounded had to do with him! He would have to flee for his life lest the crowds tear him limb from limb. As he sought refuge in the cave, he uttered words of gratitude to God, who had spared him certain death by lowering the curtains of darkness just as the wailing commenced.

From his towering perch, he saw search parties crisscrossing the valley below, and men rushing every which way with torches in their hands. At that moment he knew what an able seer this Genie really was, and that everything that had been said about her prophetic abilities was not only true, but an understatement of her actual gifts. He had misjudged her.

As time wore on, he grew drowsy, although his pursuers were still up in arms. By the time he woke from his brief slumber, the tumult had subsided, although he could hear men's voices echoing in the distance. He waited a bit longer, then rose and led his horse eastward across the pine-draped foothill. After traversing a considerable distance, he looked warily about him. Then, jumping at last into the saddle, he rode forth under cover of darkness, cradling the slender loaf like a precious treasure beneath his tattered raiment.

35

The Straw

THE MESSENGER ARRIVED SAFELY AFTER an arduous journey, the agonizing scream he had heard prior to setting out ringing in his ears the entire way. Its effects had lingered even after he reached his destination. As he stood at last before Ibn al-Nu'man, he suddenly realized that he was still wearing his tattered rags, which made for quite a laughable and pathetic sight! Ibn al-Nu'man's eyes betrayed a smile of disdain, and there were snickers from the soldiers. But none of it made any difference to him, since the marvelous sensation that had come over him when he was stripped of his peacock garb remained with him. It was the feeling of being free like Hanash Sanaani, and possibly like Abu Dharr al-Ghifari, which meant that he was as happy as Hanash—indeed, as happy as Abu Dharr!

He sat in the presence of Ibn al-Nu'man, content in his shabby attire. The happiness he felt was something that Ibn al-Nu'man—nay, the caliph himself or anyone else of their ilk—would have envied him for if they had perceived its sweetness. Indeed, if they had been allowed by the Divine Providence to perceive the precious gift they had been missing, they would have done the impossible to take it away from him.

He crouched across from the unfortunate army commander as he broke into the loaf, removed the parchment, and greedily pored over its lines. After reading what it said, he sat gazing into space for a time. When he had wakened out of his trance, he addressed the messenger imperiously as though seeing him for the first time:

"I'm afraid you'll have to go back to him!"

Baffled, the messenger made no reply until the man roared as though he had been suppressing a volcanic rage: "Go back to him!"

In the space of a fleeting moment, the precious feeling dissipated.

"Go back to him?" he murmured absently.

Waving the parchment in his face, Ibn al-Nu'man roared again, "The edge of the parchment has been burned away, and I'm missing a sentence I cannot do without!"

After several moments of silence, the messenger replied with a steely certainty, "If you had any idea what it cost me to bring you this trust, you would not ask me to go back again."

With an exasperated sigh, he added, "You may not know it, but I barely escaped with my life, and that only thanks to a miracle! Of all creatures on Earth, that woman knows best what people conceal in their hearts, but we have failed to give her her due. The least we can say about her is that she is a genie!"

"What are you saying?" murmured Ibn al-Nu'man, casting him a look of quizzical disbelief.

Not knowing whence he had mustered the courage to speak, the messenger replied, "What I am saying is that I have decided to return. However, I will not be returning to the place I just came from as you are commanding me to do. I'll be returning somewhere else—somewhere that takes me not backward, but forward!"

"Forward?" repeated Ibn al-Nu'man skeptically.

"That's right! Forward!"

After a moment's pause, the messenger expelled the words as though they had been caught in his throat, "To the East!"

"To the East?"

The messenger heaved a sigh.

"I am requesting your permission to leave."

"What's come over you?" Ibn al-Nu'man stammered. "Do you mean what you're saying?"

With a certainty that astounded even him, the messenger replied, "I never want to kill anyone again. Nor do I want to be killed for the sake of the vanities of this world!"

Tongue-tied with astonishment, the commander made no reply.

Meanwhile, the messenger continued in a tone so cold as to seem indifferent, "I thought I had come to these lands to exalt the word of God, not to weave plots or pillage the innocent in order to fill the coffers of a state treasury in which the needy have no share!"

Ibn al-Nu'man sat glaring at his messenger, his face flushed with rage. Shifting in his seat, he said at last, "Do you really intend to turn back now that God has opened before us a path to victory that we have awaited for years?"

Forcing a tense smile, he picked up the parchment and said, "Listen to what our ambassador to the Genie has to say."

Stealing a glance in his messenger's direction, the caliph read: "The tribal leaders have fallen away from the woman since her recent misstep. So now all you have to do is make haste to carry out what remains of your plan."

He stopped reading and looked intently at his interlocutor before adding, "I want you to go back to him because everything following this sentence has been consumed by the flames, and every single word in this message is worth the treasures of the world to me. But instead of doing as I ask and staying with me to witness a long-awaited triumph, you tell me suddenly that you want to go back . . . to the East!"

His gaze questioning and defiant, the messenger threw down the gauntlet. "What kind of triumph is this that we have to purchase with treachery? What kind of triumph requires us to lure someone into committing treason against the enemy as though we were some band of highway robbers, not soldiers of God?"

Ibn al-Nu'man forced another charged smile. Then, feigning an unexpected forbearance, he said, "You seem to have forgotten that we are at war, and that the capital of any war is deceit!"

"And does an expedition launched for God's sake allow for what you term 'deceit'?"

"What expedition, in your view, is not a war?" countered Ibn al-Nu'man with another contemptuous smile.

"All I know is that Ibn Yazid and those of his ilk are not doing what they do for God's sake, but in the hope of winning power."

The shadows of a crafty smile crept across Ibn al-Nu'man's features. However, he hurriedly shot back a counterargument, saying, "And who among us would not hope to win power?"

Fanning his face with the troublesome parchment as though he were shooing away flies, Ibn al-Nu'man added, "All of us seek power. It's just that most of us dream of an earthly power, while only a few of us dream of the power of heaven!"

The two men exchanged a look charged with suspicion, as though they were reading what lay concealed behind their respective masks. At length, the messenger looked away, casting his gaze into the desert expanse with the words, "The love of God is not a quest for power."

A look of derision flitted once more across the man's features.

"Oh, but it is!" he rejoined. "At least, it is in the view of fools like you, who worship at the feet of anyone who rends a garment and replaces it with rags, then goes about barefoot singing the praises of the divine love!"

Scrutinizing Ibn al-Nu'man's features in an attempt to determine whether he was speaking in seriousness or in jest, the messenger replied, "You say this because you've never experienced liberation."

"Liberation?"

Disregarding the commander's perplexed query, the messenger waxed on, "Never did I imagine that these rags would be able to free me from my self-importance, just as I never imagined that self-importance could conceal from me what I'd been searching for all my life—myself!"

The leader of the conquest eyed him curiously. As he fiddled with the miserable parchment that he had extracted from the inside of the loaf of bread, an enigmatic expression—a mixture of disbelief and contempt—passed over his features.

Just as the commander was about to speak at last, the messenger rose to his feet. Enveloped in the twilight gloom clad in his threadbare garb, he looked like a ghost that had emerged from the desert where, since time immemorial, ghosts had made their home.

Before disappearing, he uttered what sounded like a parting will and testament: "Even the straw that we despise can be a cause of deliverance!"

36

The Jizya

ONE EVENING DURING THOSE FATEFUL years when the people of
the land exchanged hit-and-run campaigns with their unin-
vited guests, everything was in a state of confusion from Barca
to Tangiers. As invariably happens when wars wear on indef-
initely, the lack of certainty about what the morrow would
bring had become a constant in people's lives. The one exception to this uncertainty, which asserted its presence in the
midst of it all as though to demonstrate a power that defied
the bloodshed and even the power of death, was the jizya.

It was this griffon, which refused to acknowledge the
changing nature of times or places, that drew a company
of four phantoms to a certain remote location one ill-fated
evening. They had come at a critical time of day which people regarded as the most evil of portents, since guests who
approached at such hours often came concealing their true
identities and designs by disguising themselves in the bodies
of human beings. Hence, before hastening to receive such
guests, people would recite protective spells and incantations
and saturate themselves in magical vapors thought to banish
evil spirits.

Having descended upon a remote encampment inhabited
by a clan that belonged originally to the Luwwata tribes, the
phantoms sought out the clan chief, whose tent was recog-
nizable by the banner that waved atop it. It was composed
of animal skins to distinguish it from the other tents, which

had been woven variously from wool or the hair of camels or goats, depending on their owners' place in the tribal hierarchy.

After coming out to receive them, the clan's chieftain ordered a tent to be set up for them in a secluded spot. Meanwhile, a number of elders hurriedly set about slaughtering animals to be served in the phantoms' honor, a task in which they were assisted by a motley entourage of elderly women and adolescent girls.

Given the absence of the tribe's horsemen, who had been taken away by the wars that raged throughout the region, the elders came forward to attend to the delegation's mounts, while the phantoms repaired to the tent for the forum to convene within. Seated together with the clan leader, the senior member of the delegation introduced himself as the trustee appointed by government officials to oversee collection of the jizya. He introduced the man next to him as the interpreter, who was authorized to decipher the cryptic symbols of language, and the other men as assistants who had come to help him carry out his mission by ensuring that right was upheld and falsehood vanquished in the event that what was owed was not forthcoming!

Following an ominous silence, the head of the delegation whispered in the interpreter's ear, "Those who hasten to slaughter animals for their guests can hardly claim not to have enough with which to pay the jizya!"

To this the chieftain replied that the animals he had had slaughtered for the jizya collector and his men, he had denied to himself and his family. He had set them aside for messengers from heaven who frequently came to the tribes' villages disguised as mere humans. Moreover, he explained, honoring the specters which the deserts graciously bestowed upon them from time to time was, in his people's belief, also a kind of jizya!

Drawing himself up, the delegation leader said, "However, the duty to feed those authorized to collect the jizya is as weighty as the duty to pay the jizya itself!"

The chieftain bowed his head. Then, with funereal solem-
nity he replied at length, "You can see for yourselves what the
last few years' drought has done to our flocks and herds, and
to every aspect of our lives in this region. Moreover, the afflictions of the ongoing war have been no less disastrous than
those of the drought."

Exchanging a meaningful glance with his men, the delegation leader replied, "Everybody uses the drought as an excuse
to avoid having to pay. As for the war, it's afflicted everyone,
the conquerors included. Besides, the jurists who established
payment of the jizya recognized neither drought nor war in
their legal code! Payment of the jizya is no less an obligation
than performing the ritual prayer, making the pilgrimage to
God's House in Mecca, fasting, or paying zakat. What zakat is
to Muslims, the jizya is to those who have chosen to purchase
the right to remain in their own religion rather than embracing the religion of the conquerors!"

When the interpreter whispered this message into his ears,
the chieftain's features brightened suddenly. Throughout the
session, he had been fiddling with small pieces of rock, which
he would cast onto the pebble-strewn soil as though he were
reading a fortune with every toss. Then he would gather them
up with his delicate fingertips and hold them in his gaunt,
claw-like fingers, clutching them tightly in his fist for a while
as though infusing them with sorrow and distress before casting them onto the ground anew. He fell still for a few moments
and the look in his eyes turned to one of curiosity. Then suddenly he burst out through the interpreter: "And how do you
know I don't believe in the conquerors' religion?"

With a superior smile, the delegation leader asked, "And
what religion might be embraced by a foreigner who speaks
nothing but the gibberish of some non-Arab people?"

The chieftain gazed intently at the rocks with which he
had been occupying himself before replying through the
interpreter, "A follower of your religion who once came here

told me that no Arab was superior to any non-Arab except insofar as he was more God-fearing!"

"And are you God-fearing?" queried his interlocutor with a sneer.

As the question was conveyed to him by the interpreter, the man nodded his head without hesitation.

"Do you pray the five daily prayers?"

The man nodded again, whereupon the jizya collector exchanged a crafty look with his myrmidons before returning to his cross-examination.

"What do you recite in each prayer?" he asked.

The chieftain clung tightly to the stones in his hands as though relying on them for assistance in conjuring a reply. Then at last, speaking again through the interpreter, the man said, "All I know is that what renders ritual prayer acceptable is one's intention!"

After a pause and more side glances among the members of the delegation, the jizya collector let forth an obnoxious guffaw to which his myrmidons responded by dissolving in a fit of laughter.

After a lengthy pause, the delegation leader dictated to his interpreter, "You may not realize how indispensable the jizya is to us. So what can you pay us to meet your obligation?"

Squeezing the stones in his fist with such force that they sounded like the grinding of teeth, the chieftain replied in desperation, "If you find anything in my possession that will speak well for me, take it!"

Once again the man and his minions exchanged surreptitious glances. Then, his features softening, he said, "I am duty-bound to inform you that jizya collectors never return from a mission empty-handed!"

The chieftain flung his rocks onto the ground as though he were flinging a handful of arrows in the jizya collector's face. "In that case," he replied, "you'll have to take me with you in pledge!"

"In pledge?" echoed the jizya collector in surprise. "We have no dealings with pledges. However, we are authorized to take something else which, in the long-standing tradition of conquerors, has always been an acceptable ransom!"

A taut silence reigned once more. The air of callousness with which the jizya collector made his rounds among the tribes as he extorted his precious spoils hung over them like an ominous cloud.

At last he said, "Tomorrow, God willing, you will be a witness to the ransom. It is not my custom to visit encampments without informing myself of the conditions of its womenfolk, and of whatever or whoever of the tribe's possessions could serve as payment if it proves impossible to collect what is owed!"

The following morning, after the chieftain had served the delegation a feast consisting of his one remaining slaughter animal—the animal he had set aside for his guests—soldiers stormed the tent, seized three girls, and led them away to a caravan of slave women stationed in the distance in preparation to set out for the East. The girls were the host's only daughters—everything he had in this world.

37

Foundlings
AH 82/704 CE

THE GENIE RETREATED INTO HER bottle for days. However, what Ibn Yazid had done didn't surprise her, perhaps because of her conviction that the offspring of outsiders was bound to be an "intrigue" of some sort, no matter how deftly she may have deluded herself into seeing nothing but his beauty and virtuous qualities. In any case, every offspring is by nature an intrigue. How much truer would this be of the offspring of strangers? Wasn't Yuhal an intrigue? Wasn't Yujay an intrigue?

Isn't all progeny, in essence, an intrigue woven by the hidden Realm to lure us to our destinies while, at the same time alleviating the suffering brought by the end that awaits us? Children don't exist to give us life, but to put us to death, and their births are merely a trap, albeit the loveliest trap imaginable in every mother's life. She had just forgotten this fact, as every mother is wont to do, and pretended to have stumbled upon a precious find every time she had a child. Then, when her body's springs had run dry and the milk in her breasts had ceased to flow, she had had no choice but to quench her thirst for offspring by clinging to the children the Fates had placed in her path. She didn't even know what it was that had so charmed her in the boy Khalid. Was it a supposed bravery with which she had arbitrarily invested him? Was it some imagined beauty she had wanted him to have?

Perhaps all of this had simply been her way of justifying to herself her desire to adopt, of satisfying her hunger

167

to acquire more offspring not only of flesh and blood, but of some substance loftier than flesh and blood. It was as though she had expected them to be playthings of sorts, and not the very embodiment of danger, although the danger they had posed had not surprised her. Khalid, as the most recent intruder, was more dangerous than his two brothers, although in the end they were all intruders!

What was it about them that so captivated her? Why did she feel a need for sons in the first place?

What force drew her to offspring whom she knew full well she could not rely on either to realize an aim or achieve happiness? Had she sought them out after the manner of women who see themselves merely as war-time ammunition factories, while forgetting that wars would not have broken out in the first place if they had not so generously provided them with the ammunition they needed? How could she have forgotten that with her mystical gifts she had achieved for her people what other women had failed to achieve with their wombs? Why was she so captivated by the "fruit of the womb," which had been granted to mothers who lacked the gifts that come from the Realms of the Unseen yet had nothing to boast of but the fruits of their bodies, when she had received something far greater—spiritual vision?

Instead of being content with her destiny as a seer, why did she strive to go on acquiring offspring for whom she had no need? Why was she struggling with such determination to remain a female like all other females, a woman like all other women, while despising the treasures of the Realm everlasting, and panting like a fool after the mirage of ephemeral wealth? What was the meaning of this stab in the back from someone for whom she had done nothing but good, embracing him as a son when what she should have done was place his neck on the leather execution mat and order him beheaded from the very first day of his captivity? After all, he had approached her on the battlefield with sword unsheathed in order to take her life!

Was this betrayal not the punishment she merited for having adopted a foundling so undeserving? The teachings of the lost law had warned against foundlings, saying, "O descendants of Adam! Whatever you find on the path, you may pick up and benefit from with one exception: another human being!"

According to the Lost Book, the Fates are unjust to no one. When they cast someone out, they do so for a reason—in punishment for a sin known only to those in the Realms of the Unseen. Therefore, when we pick up someone who has fallen, we defy the Fates. We nullify the effect of a deserved punishment. We interfere in the divine will by issuing a pardon we have no right to grant to sinners whose fall only came about in order to teach them lessons and to purify them through chastisement. Through our interference we overturn the verdict, redeeming sinners unbeknownst to us and bearing the punishment on their behalf due to our ignorance of the truth about the sin that had rendered the chastisement necessary. Thus, we pay the price for having purchased an unknown transgression.

In this case, we cannot condemn the ingratitude we receive in return for the kindness we may have shown, since ingratitude is simply the night having its say against us for stepping in to redeem a creature that had been vowed to destruction.

Furthermore, Ibn Yazid had been within his rights to "stab" her because it was not he who was stabbing her, but rather the Realms of the Unseen, which were acting through him to punish her for her sin against them. It was the Realms of the Unseen that had broken his sword in order to help him atone for sins of his own. They had delivered him into her hands, not so that she could protect him, but so that she could carry out the remainder of his rightful punishment.

But instead, she had shown tolerance and violated the laws of war—indeed, the very nature of things, thereby provoking the Realms of the Unseen to anger. They had granted him the power to forsake her so that in his betrayal, she would discern a message—that however foolish Its doings may appear

169

to human beings, the Unknown is not engaged in the business of foolishness and will not be mocked!

Since the sin that had rendered her a victim was her own, she had no right to cast blame on the boy. After all, he was nothing but the messenger from the Realms of the Unseen. By adopting him as a son in what she had thought to be an act of charity, she had taken on a punishment that he should have suffered himself, and which she would now have to share with him—nay, borrow from him in its entirety and bear on his behalf!

She had only herself to blame, because the alien son had not betrayed her; she had betrayed herself. Disdaining the law of the ancestors, she had picked up from the roadside that very "find" which the Lost Law had forbidden her to touch.

How she despised herself now. In a fit of rage, she had summoned her sons and had them stand as witnesses to what their adopted brother had done. Then she had subjected him to a grueling interrogation which, as she had realized when she appealed to the teachings of the lost Anhi, had been futile in the greater scheme of things. Though lost, the ancient Scripture remained alive and would go on living as long as it continued to whisper in the hearts of succeeding generations. It was not her place now to busy herself with interrogations, since what awaited her was too momentous for her to be wasting time searching for a truth that, as she had known all along, could be found nowhere but in the Scriptures.

38

Needs

FOR SOME TIME, SPECTERS OF the oppressed, the needy, and the wronged had hovered around the haircloth tent of "the wounded lion," whose patrols generally kept them at bay. On very rare occasions, however, certain fortunate individuals would be allowed to appear before the emir for their needs to be met.

On one such occasion, the chamberlain's heart had softened toward a certain wretch who had been circling about for days on end, begging to be granted an audience with the emir. He faced a dire situation to which no one but the ruler, he believed, would be able to find a solution. If the truth be told, the chamberlain's lenience on this occasion was not so much due to a softening of the heart as it was to an event which everyone had seen as an auspicious omen, a prelude to their deliverance from an internment that had lasted for an entire five years. Following the invading army's defeat in its last battle with al-Kahina, the surviving soldiers had retreated to an isolated crossroads where they expected to wait for a brief period of time, only to find their enforced stay wearing on for years on end.

At last, however, a messenger had come bearing the glad tidings that the long-awaited rations and reinforcements would soon arrive from the East, thereby enabling the army to resume its westward advance. It was a report at which the entire camp rejoiced, causing everyone to heave a collective sigh of relief. It was as though they had been brought back from the dead after having been left in what felt like an endless limbo. They no longer belonged to the East, which had expelled them, nor did they yet belong in the West, where they had anticipated establishing a new home.

The question now was: Had the heart of the people's leader also softened in his joy over the glad tidings? Perhaps it had, though not to the extent that he could open the door wide to receive the unfortunate because he simply lacked the wherewithal to meet their needs. Perhaps for this reason, the chamberlain would have to entreat the emir to show compassion for the needy man in question, since only then could he hope that God would open the door of His mercy to him and reward him for what he had done with one of the two paradises: the paradise of military victory, which would reunite him with his family at last, or the paradise of martyrdom, which would reunite him with his Lord. For he was among those who believed that the mercy we receive from Heaven will be commensurate with the mercy we have shown on Earth.

The chamberlain went in to plead with his emir, certain that no one but he would be able to persuade him to undertake an action that would either benefit him in his relationship with his Lord or win him prosperity in his earthly life. Indeed, chamberlains are their emirs' guardians. In this capacity, a chamberlain can dictate to a ruler what his courtiers, ministers, wives, or even paramours could not. In short, the chamberlain is the emir's conscience, closer to him than his very jugular vein. For this reason, an emir may be brought to ruin by a chamberlain with evil intentions, since he alone has the power to tempt him to evil. Conversely, a chamberlain may bring a ruler the most blessed of fortunes, since he alone has the ability to make charity and virtue beautiful in the ruler's eyes, thereby leading him to felicity and salvation!

The chamberlain pled with his emir on that day to receive a man who was weak and oppressed, a man who had both worn him down and won his compassion with his importunity and determination. The emir had no choice but to accede to the chamberlain's will. Before receiving the petitioner, however, he inquired as to whether this scion of foreigners had mastered the tongue in which *al-furqan*—the decisive Word—had been revealed. He couldn't help but smile when the chamberlain replied jokingly, "He knows it as well as his fellow foreigners, who claim to have mastered it, only to demonstrate that their 'mastery' goes no further than the first half-sentence that comes out of their mouths, then evaporates immediately thereafter as they inadvertently prattle away in their own gibberish!"

The chamberlain was happy with himself for having taken the hand of someone who was weak and oppressed. Before withdrawing from his emir's presence, he expressed his gratitude with a flood of prayers that the Divine Providence might grant him success in spreading the call to Truth, and victory over the hordes of polytheists in the anticipated expedition.

As the chamberlain exited, the interpreter entered accompanied by a gaunt man in his fifth or sixth decade with gnarled limbs and fingers so skeletal they resembled the claws of a wild animal. The man's eyes emitted a glint in which Ibn al-Nuʿman discerned an excruciating pain. After scrutinizing him in silence, the emir looked evasively aside. He thought back for the thousandth time on the jurists' teaching that the soul most beloved to God is one who does not withhold from those in need, even when those in need fail to realize what this largesse has cost him. After all, the indigent are ignorant of the fact that their benefactors are hardly able to meet their own needs, still less those of others. The place occupied by those whom people perceive as being capable of meeting others' needs is not some impenetrable fortress that exudes authority. On the contrary, it is a snare for a helpless human being who has no say over his own fate, since he does not see with his own eyes, hear with his own ears, or speak with his own tongue, nor is he capable of changing himself of his own

173

volition. He is not a sultan, but a wretch saddled with a power that is not truly his, a vacuous bogeyman who may serve well as a camouflage, but cannot address people's necessities or anything of the sort.

As for those actually in a position to address such necessities, they form a chain which begins with those closest to the sultan or emir, such as the chamberlain or those of similar rank, then descends to the bottom rung of the ladder, where no one would be suspected of having any power in the least. In short, those who are truly capable of meeting needs are the servants, not their masters! The chamberlain had appealed to the emir to receive the unfortunate creature who now stood before him.

The chamberlain had taken this step not because he lacked the ability to meet the man's need himself, but simply because he required an official authorization from the emir to do so—a decree that would lend his action a legitimacy that could only be conferred by his idolized benefactor.

Had he not been embarrassed to tamper with the norms that governed this foolish state of affairs, the emir would have shouted at the chamberlain, "Why do you always insist on barging in on me with people you know very well I have no way of helping when you could just as well have spared me by taking care of things on my behalf?"

He thought back on the way in which, before he set out westward with his troops, Abd al-Aziz ibn Marwan, Governor of Egypt, had instructed him to take good care of a relative of his who was serving in his army and how, without hesitation, he had retorted, "Rather than instructing me to take care of your relative, you should instruct this relative of yours to take care of me!"

He knew full well that those in leadership were actually in greater need of care than the subordinates in the leaders' charge! In order to meet others' needs, the person in power would have to be what he was incapable of being—his own master—instead of a mere shadow of the true authority. In this case, the emir would need to take on the role of the subordinate who had received the order—such as the chamberlain, for example, or others close to the leader—by carrying the order out. Then he would need to play the roles of all the heroes in the accursed chain from top to bottom! But would a person in a position of authority be willing to disguise himself as someone on the lowest rung of the ladder in order to meet the needs at hand? Would he be willing to descend from his throne and clothe himself in the spirit of the servants who by nature enjoyed the coveted right to meet the needs at hand—a right that had always been their own unique possession and prize?

39

Wounds to the Spirit

THROUGH THE INTERPRETER, THE MAN related how Ibn al-Nuʿmanʾs soldiers had seized his three daughters and led them away by force, in place of the jizya that the drought had rendered him unable to pay. After telling his story, he asked, "Does your Scripture—the one whose teachings youʾve come to spread by killing our men—allow the jizya to be extracted from someone who has embraced Islam, and who now performs the ritual prayers and pays the zakat?"

After studying the man for some time, Ibn al-Nuʿman asked him about the *suras*, or chapters of the Quran that are to be recited as part of the ritual prayers. In reply, the man said that he had been doing his best to memorize the shorter *suras* so that he could recite them in his prayers. Then, as if as an afterthought, the man asked through the interpreter, "Didnʾt you teach us that intention is the mainstay of the ritual prayer? Donʾt your legal scholars say that utterance of the two testimonies of faith is sufficient evidence that one has entered your religion?"

The emir gazed at the man curiously without saying a word.

The bereaved father went on quickly to complain, "At this stage in my life, every loss feels like a permanent one that could never be reversed or compensated for. Once one is past the age of fifty, itʾs difficult, if not impossible, to replace friends. So how much more difficult and even impossible would it be with oneʾs own children?"

After a moment's pause, the man suddenly broke into a rapid monologue in his musical gibberish, which the interpreter was hard-pressed to convey into the language of *al-furqan*.

He said, "In our language we refer to offspring as *quruh al-ruh*—'wounds to the spirit.' Yet we seek them out despite knowing how deadly they are. Has the venerable emir ever experienced 'wounds to the spirit'?"

The man fell silent for a moment before asking, "Isn't it madness for us to take pride in having offspring that we know full well to be 'wounds to the spirit' in the sense that, if they were absent from our world, we could no longer bear to live?"

He grew quiet again, and silence reigned. At length he stammered, "All I want as my years draw to a close is for you to do whatever you can to restore to me the life-force that I lost with the disappearance of my *quruh al-ruh*!"

His heart moved with pity, Ibn al-Nu'man shifted repeatedly in his seat before addressing the bereaved old man, saying, "It wasn't I who established the custom of taking young women away from their families in return for the jizya. Rather, it was established by the commanders who preceded me to these parts. But if a custom prevails for a period of time, it becomes habit, and habit quickly becomes second nature in a society that's embraced the religion of war. As for me personally, I have avoided living in cities for fear of falling captive to these very customs. As you will note, I refused to live in Kairouan, or claim my share of the booty, or take concubines. I didn't want to give myself a taste of luxury, lest wealth be my demise as it has been for so many. At the same time, it is not for me to deprive soldiers of booty they have earned with their blood, since the law of war is a religion unto itself. It is a religion that does not recognize the religion proper and condones injustices which the religion proper forbids. The greatest of commanders will be brought down not by enemy soldiers, but by his own troops if he appeals to the letter of the religion in this regard. Nevertheless, assuming they have not left in the caravan headed eastward, I will spare no effort to restore to you your lost *quruh al-ruh*." In fact, Ibn al-Nu'man did everything in his power to recover the ill-fated spoils. But alas, his efforts came too late, as the caravan that had taken the slave girls into their various places of exile had set out two days earlier.

40

The East

THE SEER PLUNGED INTO THE depths of her solitude, seeking refuge in its darkness. She cut herself off this time not to plead with her visions and prophetic messages, but to cross-examine them. She needed to interrogate a nightmare in which she had seen herself slain. Had the dream alarmed her? Had it shaken her to die? No, not at all! She had seen herself dead numerous times before. However, she had felt no relief upon waking from her nightmares. She had not rejoiced at coming back alive like fools who, after being raised from death in a dream, view this return as a kind of second birth. Only the foolish celebrate being alive or rejoice at being restored from death in a dream. She understood, of course, that the vast majority of people could never imagine that there was no difference between what we term life and death. They could never imagine that what appears to them to be life is simply one side of a dull copper coin in which presence and absence are paired. No one knows which side is life and which is death, and no one knows the true nature of either side, not even priests, the artful and shrewd, or those who have been granted abundant knowledge of the Realms Unseen. At the same time, such individuals constantly wonder whether this side to which we cling is actually the ugly side that we fear and refer to as death, while what awaits us after death might actually be the life we long and strive for. If this were not so, why would all the Scriptures, including the long-lost Anhi, affirm this paradox, tirelessly singing the praises of the Realm one enters at death? The praiseworthiness of this other Realm is evidenced by the fact that it is the only dimension governed by that miraculous entity which human beings have failed since the beginning of Time to cultivate in their earthly soil: justice!

If justice were not alien to Earth—this dimension in which we take such pride and which we are so eager to hold onto, forgetting what afflictions are brought by all of its gifts (or what we deem to be gifts)—people would not have found it so impossible to cultivate this magical plant. This barren land which we call home may provide sustenance for the perishable body, but it could never yield nourishment for the soul. Justice alone is fit nourishment for the immortal treasure known as the spirit. This is why justice is never obtained, nor could it ever flourish, on the mortal face of the rusting copper coin. Similarly, justice would never have chosen the coin's other face as a place to grow if it were not a realm worthy of trust. Indeed, it is the homeland of spirit. Were it not, eternity would not reign there!

Earthly justice is a pipe dream, and those who aspire to achieve it in this ephemeral wasteland are truly mad.

The Seer recognized now, as she always had, how foolish it had been of her to attempt to establish a monument to a sprite so inaccessible to those in the Lowlands. She had striven to bring her down from her Unseen eternal Realms in hopes of investing her, against her will, with an earthly identity. Hence, she had no reason to be surprised at the ignominious defeat she had suffered in a quest that she now knew to have been a childish one, since the justice she had attempted to cultivate has no home among humans. On the contrary, it can only be achieved in some other dimension beyond Earth's frontiers.

The most recent in a series of disasters she had faced in regard to the absence of justice was the visit she had received the day before from a certain tribal delegation. The delegation members had come before her with a bitter complaint concerning the accursed jizya with which the invaders had shackled the region's inhabitants, particularly the practice of kidnapping their daughters and leading them away to serve as concubines in the lands of the East despite their families' having embraced the alien religion. What could she have done to support them or recover their offspring? How was she to exact revenge on people who made a profession of igniting wars when, as everyone knows, in wartime all is lawful, and the copies of the Quran raised high on their spear tips were nothing but an excuse to amass blood-drenched plunder?

After all she had endured and witnessed over the years, did it make any sense to believe that there was hope of erecting a monument to justice on this star-crossed side of the rusty copper coin? For so long she had made excuses for herself in an attempt to make light of her failures, waiting for the Realms of the Unseen to rush to her aid with a prophecy by which she could quench her thirst for revenge and compensate for the years she had wasted. But it had all been in vain. Consequently, the nightmarish vision had not robbed her of her senses. On the contrary, it had given her a glimpse of her deliverance.

The night before she had had a dream that portended a freedom she had been after for long, long years. At last the Realms of the Unseen had willed to grant her release. So by what right did she describe it as a "nightmare" when its content had held out to her the fulfillment of a long-cherished dream? She had not been in a deep slumber but rather in a state somewhere between sleeping and waking, which meant that the vision she had seen could be deemed a trustworthy prophecy.

For some reason known only to the Realms of the Unseen, she was holding her adopted son Ibn Yazid, once again a helpless infant clinging to her breast, as she fled from a secret terror that pursued her across unknown regions, through thickets and up and down rugged pathways. She held him close in her protective embrace as though she feared that the hidden force pursuing her would snatch him away.

At length she came to an imposing mansion atop a high hill crowned with the mists of dusk. After searching frantically for an entrance, she suddenly found herself inside the eerie palace. She roamed its corridors until, entering a spacious hall ringed by ornate pillars similar to the ones in the great mosque she had seen during her advance on Kairouan, she encountered a solemn specter whose features she was unable to discern in the darkness. He gazed at her curiously, or so it seemed to her, as though he wanted to reassure her that he would protect her from the foes who were on her trail. Inspired by this sense of reassurance to place her charge in his care, she presented him with the infant Ibn Yazid. The specter took the child with an air of gratitude evidenced by a mysterious smile that passed over his features.

However, when she took another look at the gift she had placed in the specter's hands, she discovered that it was not a baby, but her head!

It was her severed head, with disheveled hair, bloodied face, and eyes that stared into the void with a look of grieved bewilderment.

As the specter received the head from her with a grateful bow, she suddenly discovered, in a flash of inspiration, that the figure looming before her was none other than the King of the Arabs, seated there in a Dimension Beyond veiled in the shadows of legend, at once guardian over the repository of evils and the coffer of wisdom. Referred to by some as the gateway of the Ennead, it has at times dealt death, and at other times graced humankind with life-giving prophecies. Through this frenzied pendulum swing borrowed from the cycles of the seasons, it demonstrates the absence of any truth beyond the scope of the two opposites. Known as "the East," it is a snare of seduction; otherwise, how could it have lured into its realm even the sun, which has chosen it from among all the corners of the Universe as the birthplace for each new day?

41

The Bleeding of the Spirit

TO THE CARETAKER OF THE sanctum of the East (who had set out for the four corners of the earth with hordes brought forth from some hidden bottomless repository), she went bearing in her arms the vile plot. Thinking that there was no way to extinguish the flames of war among the world's nations without forging the ties of a brotherhood that she had embraced as her religion, she had taken him in as her own son. From this religion of hers she had woven a fabric into which she had once incorporated the Greeks and Europeans. Moreover, since she belonged to a nation which had exalted the female as its object of worship since time immemorial, she was unwilling to relinquish her religion. It was through the feminine that the Realms of the Unseen had rescued the nations from the madness of a man thirsty for murder, who would have put himself to death as well if he had found no one else to kill.

So, had she been betrayed by the intuition on which she had relied for so long?

No, her intuition had not betrayed her. On the contrary, it was the faithful interpreter of events as it always had been. It was Intuition that had led her to the stronghold that had first ignited the sparks of war. It had led her to the soothsayer stationed on the throne of the East, holding an effigy which she had thought to be a child worthy of serving as a talisman that would engender peace between them, only to learn that the "deal" she had concluded had been a losing proposition—on her side, at least—since Khalid ibn Yazid, the child on whom she had pinned her hopes, had left her in the lurch to become the cause of her downfall instead of the instrument of her salvation.

This was the first message the prophetic nightmare had conveyed. However, it had also contained another treasure which she dared not disregard. In the vision, the gift of the head stood out as a puzzle that resisted interpretation. At the same time, it promised to yield an abundant storehouse of knowledge if she dug as deeply and valiantly as the situation required. And dig she did. She held lonely vigil for days, challenging the hidden realities to make themselves known. She refrained from food and wore nothing but seamless garments.

In her quest to grasp the truth which the Realms of the Unseen had encrypted in the metaphor of the severed head, she veiled herself from others. She strained her spiritual gifts to the limit; had she not persevered, they would have failed her. The head is the fount of earthly governance, the receptacle of wisdom from which judgments proceed, be they those that give life or those that deal death. If such a tightly sealed urn containing the cryptic symbols of rulings and edicts had fallen as booty into another's hands—severed from its source, washed in its own blood—this could only point to a serious error in the manner in which it had been put to use.

As for the act of picking it up and offering it as a gift to an enemy—not under duress, but voluntarily—this could only point to the relinquishment of a right, the surrender to a destiny which, in the tradition of prophecy, meant that she alone had brought about her defeat. What did this mean?

She plunged still deeper into regions unknown which, before long, yielded a spontaneous moment in which, overcome by a sense of utter futility, she relaxed, determined to let go of everything, including her very existence. As this occurred, the pristine truth stood forth in all its brilliance. Her eyes opened at last, and she marveled at how accessible the truth had been all along, wondering how it could have eluded her throughout that painful, frenzied, days-long duel.

Indeed, the truth was that when she succumbed to the wicked urge to destroy her blessed realm with her own hands, demolishing the throne of her glories of her own accord, she had betrayed herself. It was true that her people had forsaken her. However, the reason they had done so was that she herself had unwittingly forsaken them. In a fit of madness, she had demolished their fortresses and their blessed urban centers, burned their crops, and scattered their families. In so doing, she had demonstrated that when those endowed with visions are defeated, they are not defeated by aliens, but by their own actions. On that day, she had rendered judgment against herself. Perhaps she had simply not wanted to go on combating futility on this rusty side of the coin of ill-fortune, and the Realms of the Unseen had granted her wish.

Only then did she realize that she had long been entertaining the notion of exiting this world. However, she had been ignoring this because of her belief in the teachings of the lost Scripture, which urge believers to bear the burden of life in this world for as long as they can, knowing that a lengthy sojourn on Earth is an opportunity to tame the spirit in preparation for an indestructible joy that can only be attained through deliverance from slavery and release from the trap!

Had she committed an outrage against herself, unwittingly bringing about her own demise? Or had the muse that had inspired her for so long forsaken her on that day when, speaking through her, it issued the senseless commands that shook the pillars of her reign and heralded its end?

She had always questioned those inner whisperings and had done her best to defeat them. However, the inner whisperer is a malevolent guide that will not rest until it has driven its victim to surrender. This is what it had done to her predecessors who, exhausted from roaming across endless deserts, would turn aside, pillowing their heads on an empty water skin under the open sky, and go to sleep to grant their souls a measure of peace.

Exhaustion is a bleeding of the spirit, and for those whose spirits have bled out, there is no hope of survival.

42

The Abode
Tripoli, early in the month of Dhu al-Hijjah, AH 83/705 CE

ONCE THE REINFORCEMENTS ARRIVED, IBN al-Nu'man continued his westward advance toward Tripoli. Upon reaching the
outskirts of the city, he encamped with his army along heights
garbed in the pine trees that had survived Dahiya's scorched-
earth campaign. The hills overlooked the remaining edifices
of the age-old coastal city of Leptis Magna. Established by
the Europeans at the mouth of Wadi Lebda, its rich remains
and luxurious structures bore witness to a passing glory. He
had encamped near these ancient ruins in hopes of discerning
how they had endured in their feverish, mortal struggle with
time. He had then striven to leave his mark on a remote land
bridge through his opulent mansions.

Only now did he realize that he could not rely on these
edifices of his, which he had not constructed in a quest for
immortality as he had once imagined, or chosen to imagine,
but rather as a source of mere amusement. He had erected
them to console himself in his affliction and to give himself
something to work toward in a time of unbearable anticipation. His purpose in building them had been to prove to
himself that he was capable of breathing out life and taming
dreams, for if living on that bridge had brought a kind of isolation, then defeat had brought isolation double-fold.

Now, given the unambiguous signs he had discerned in the
abandoned edifices of the Europeans, he wondered whether
the edifices he had constructed in a remote outpost had ever

been anything but a mere crossroads. As such, they were the true word that would succeed him when he crossed over just as everyone before him had crossed over, and as everyone who succeeded him would cross over. Perhaps what he ought to rely on was his quest to lure people in droves into the religion of Truth, even if he had to drive them into Paradise in chains. He had always believed that people would only enter the gardens of bliss if they were dragged there in chains. Otherwise, why had the apostles and their followers resorted to the sword in order to spread their messages?

Every morning he would descend the hill and wander the ruins of those legendary marble structures. He would steal into empty dwellings and explore streets paved with stones so neatly cut, it was as though those who had once passed down them had only left for a brief rest and would soon awaken to carry on with their day-to-day lives. He frequented luxurious, spring-fed baths that waited to receive the town notables accompanied by their wives, where their feverish, even lustful, yearning for immersion could be quenched to the full.

In the course of his circuit, he would contemplate the proud statues, sculpted from the whitest of marble, that stood at every corner of the city. Vast in its reach, the metropolis stretched as far as the eye could see, its easternmost edge marked by a magnificent amphitheater.

Statues of gods, goddesses, heroes, kings, and queens loomed here and there as though standing watch over a city which for reasons unknown had been abandoned by its people and left as a trust to those who would come after them. Upon their departure, they had taken with them even their tombs. Had it not been for these majestic ruins, no one would have believed they had ever passed this way.

This was the fabled entity in which the strangers from the other shore had sought to embody and preserve their wisdom. However, time had forsaken them, as it forsakes everyone who relies on the construction of edifices as a means of achieving immortality. All that remained of their good fortune were the ruins now inhabited by their spirits which, in the last analysis, were the only booty they could claim. Only after it was too late did they perceive the astuteness of the place's inhabitants who, having pledged never to seek shelter behind walls, had made sport of every intruder who came to establish an urban civilization, preferring to live out their mortal days roaming the inland expanses. Indeed, because they had borne witness to the falsehood inherent in all ephemeral creations, time had always come to their rescue.

Ibn al-Nu'man himself belonged to a community of phantoms that wandered the wilderness, who were accustomed to tightening their grip on fortresses but were wary of being imprisoned within them. Hence, he had refused to take up residence in Kairouan lest he succumb to the lure of material comfort, whose danger to a soul already prone to evil he knew all too well.

He had been reproached for this decision by his subordinates. They had reminded him that the city's founder was the martyred Uqba, who had dedicated it to his Lord and purged it of snakes, scorpions, and wild beasts in preparation for constructing a mosque where the Muslims could conduct ritual prayers. They insisted that Ibn al-Nu'man spend the night in the city in order to conciliate the spirit of a companion who had given his life for the cause of God. However, he did not do as he had been bidden, certain that the entire Earth was the sanctuary of God, and that no land is better than any other except insofar as those who inhabit it live in godly fear. Most of those residing in Kairouan at that time had until only recently been polytheists, while believers firmly established in Islam still made up only a small minority of the city's population, and he doubted his ability to stand firm in his faith were he to settle there.

43

The Offering

STILL IN HER PLACE OF hermitage, al-Kahina heaved a sigh of relief in celebration of the finale which, in the tradition of the wise, would be more honorable than the beginning. Nothing remains after prophecy but to pass the true understanding of the message on to succeeding generations.

In pursuit of such understanding, she had remained in a state of feverish confusion for days and even weeks. Perhaps this understanding would be the final word conveyed by her prolonged sojourn on Earth. What riches can be found within the final outcome of a sojourn as illumined by hope as it is tainted by suffering! Perhaps true understanding consists in the recognition that something is coming to its end. Recognition is a panacea, an acceptance of what the soul refuses to acknowledge in its never-ending battle with the specter of impermanence. Recognition dispels illusion, and does away with the temptation to grasp for more. It is a bargain with the messenger of Fate (which is itself the Law), an unconditional acceptance of its will. It is only through recognition that we become willing to relinquish our demands in our pact with Fate; herein lies another of its virtues.

As we near the end of this painful journey whose final outcome no one can imagine when he takes his first step along the path, what meaning can we find in our most sacred beliefs if we have never overcome our own helplessness? Where is the truth in a teaching when we who have authorized ourselves to convey it have never even mastered ourselves? By what right do we permit ourselves to decree something over which we have had no control even during our lifetimes, still less when we are counted among the dead?

She had often debated with herself over what endures and what passes away. At last, however, she had concluded that everything passes away except what human beings knit with their life-stories and weave with their breaths during their years on Earth. Everything else is subject to the same Fate that had decreed a long life for her, a life through which she hoped to have left a mark with her mortal sacrifice, since in this sacrifice lay her final testimony. It was her hope that this testimony would be transformed into a lesson, and that this lesson would be inherited by the nation to whom she had devoted her existence. The only thing she would have left to give them after her departure was the grace of being guided by the message inherent in this sacrifice.

As for the offspring on which she had depended in bolstering the underpinnings of brotherhood among the nations, she would know how to protect them from the invaders' thirst for bloodshed. Like a marionette, every human enterprise is controlled by hidden strings which, when pulled skillfully, can tame it, however savage it may seem. However, if she failed to locate the strings behind the bizarre afflictions that had befallen her state and whose ominous clouds had yet to dissipate—like a curse sent down in punishment for a sin committed by those who had come long before—she would doubt her clairvoyant powers.

According to the lost Scripture, Anhi, the punishment for the sins of our forebears remains a hidden debt which awaits payment by those who succeed them down to the seventh generation. However, the debt does not remain hidden; it hangs over the entire nation as befits a verdict handed down by the will of the gods. Indeed, the curse will afflict anyone who has the temerity to come to the people's aid. This is what happened to Idkran in the days spoken of in legends, and to Yugurtha after him. Perhaps the fate met by Kusaila in more recent times had also been evidence of the truth of this principle. Now she too was being haunted by the curse, which had no intention of releasing her until she accepted her fate as the required offering. It was a fate she would readily accept if she could redeem people who had inherited afflictions passed down from one generation to the next. For a blasphemy against the gods will linger beyond the seventh generation— nay, perhaps beyond the seventieth—unless it is atoned for by a blood offering of great moment.

44

Migration

As Ibn al-Nu'man moved from place to place, he wondered what it is that makes people abandon their homelands and explore the horizons. If the choice had been his, he would never have budged from where he was. He would never have chosen anywhere else as a substitute for the place of his birth.

Ibn al-Nu'man had once asked Hanash Sanaani what captivated him about migration, to which he had replied, "First, it's a way of emulating the Seal of the Messengers. And secondly, I migrate to be free. If human beings had been born to stay in one place, we would never have left our mothers' bellies!"

Are we really only born to flee from our families, from our homes, even from ourselves if we can find nothing else to flee from? Do we flee in pursuit of dreams? Or do we invent dreams as a way of lending meaning to our flight?

Was exploring the horizons truly a form of salvation as Hanash believed it to be, or was it merely a quest for plunder? Weary of remaining in one place, his ancestors had plied the expanses of the vast peninsula from the Hijaz northward toward the "Land of Blackness," as the ancients used to refer to Mesopotamia, and southward across Yemen and Ethiopia.

When, weary of travel, they settled in this place or that, they had not been content to remain where they were, but had roamed the lands of neighboring tribes. Hadn't he also moved about from one region to another, taking up residence in some clan's encampments only to abandon them for the tents of another tribe, even though he was not obliged to do so by the necessities of trade or flocks in need of fresh pastures?

What was the difference between this and answering the call of the Unknown within his soul? When there were no distant horizons to explore, he would make circles around himself, justifying this feverish restlessness as a way of dispelling a worry that whispered to his soul. Wasn't this inner whispering something he had inherited from forebears who were said to have been inclined by nature to be nomadic from time immemorial, and who only succumbed to the appeal of a sedentary life in response to the women who had lured them into a prison known as "place"?

He tried to imagine what might have happened to the mission to spread Islam had it not been furthered by migration. Was it not a sufficient boast that by virtue of migration alone, truth had triumphed over falsehood, and God had led polytheists to faith? In its absence, he might well have inherited nothing but error from his forebears, and never reached the place where he found himself now: dwelling in distant regions, spurning his selfish whims for the sake of leading alien nations to the paradise of Truth. Would he—he who of all his comrades most preferred the settled life—have been willing to endure such hardship had it not been for his belief that the mission to call others to the religion of Truth was a worthy consolation?

If he had not dedicated all he had to the cause of God from the time he first set out, could he have borne the bitterness of defeat, then waited, in a war whose unpredictable nature he knew all too well, to be martyred after the manner of the many Companions who had died for the cause before him? Wouldn't martyrdom be a sufficient reward for his having sacrificed a stable life in the place that had grown so comfortable and familiar? Staying in one place had become almost second nature—a second nature alien to the instincts of his forebears, and even those of their forefather Adam, who, no sooner had he been expelled from God's homeland, took up the life of a wayfarer. As the successor of successors, he had no cause to grieve, for he had gone forth to defend the word of God and, with this ransom, to atone for inherited sin and recover the paradise lost.

When he reached Tripoli in his westward advance, Ibn al-Nu'man stationed himself outside the city walls. He passed other cities as well, not stopping until he and his army overlooked the outskirts of Kairouan. There, on the periphery of this metropolis where the first Islamic call to prayer had been sounded in North Africa—indeed, on the entire African content—a surprise awaited him.

45

The Intrigue

AFTER CROSS-EXAMINING HER MUSE—Intuition—for long hours in her place of retreat, she summoned her milk-son to appear before her.

She had tamed her indignation quite heroically, though she only managed to quiet her rage after a painful battle. After all, forgiving betrayal entails the bloodiest duel one will ever have with oneself. It was a duel she would have lost had she not put to death all feeling in herself by appealing to the Realm of what she liked to call "the indefinite future." By placing the confrontation in this foggy domain, she sutured her bleeding wound. She had no regrets, for the indefinite future never disappoints its devotees.

What did she stand to gain by subjecting this son, who had only recently been introduced into her family through the sacred milk ritual, to an interrogation over the plot he had hatched against her? By adopting him, she had chosen to deliver him from destruction. Furthermore, remaining silent about the sins of a transgressor is the most powerful means of canceling out the effects of those sins. Likewise, making excuses for children who have slipped and fallen is the best way to win them back from their waywardness, while putting them on trial is liable to alienate them and ensure their loss!

Her aim was to win him over as her son, since this would be the first step on the path to the brotherhood whose foundations she had pledged to lay among the world's peoples. This had remained her cherished dream, although the tribal elders mocked the notion, since they were persuaded that people are essentially one another's mortal foes. During the respite which she had dubbed "the indefinite future," she had been able to arrive at a clearer understanding of what he had done. She realized she would have committed the same sin against her benefactor if she had been in similar circumstances. He had simply done what would win his people victory in their war against the foe. It had been a show of loyalty to his own countrymen, a means of lifting up the community into which he had been born. However treasonous it may have appeared to the other side, it had, from his perspective, been in fulfillment of a duty. By what right could she accuse him of an act of perfidy which, by ordinary standards, would be deemed an act of heroism? Yes, it had been a violation of a covenant. However, the covenant he had violated had been sealed in a situation over which he had had no control.

She was grateful for the Law she had adopted as her religion and which dictated that she place every difficulty that defied resolution in the safekeeping of "the indefinite future." She left judgment to the Realms of the Unseen, whose wisdom required her to consult the passing of the days for understanding. Now she was reaping the fruit of her patience, as the Realms of the Unseen rewarded her by enabling her to regain a son who, from the perspective of Time, was still a mere infant in view of how recently he had joined the family.

She clung for strength to the force that none can conquer—forgiveness—and forgiveness rushed to her rescue. In fact, Ibn Yazid's behavior began betraying hints of that veiled anguish—also known as pangs of conscience—which forgiveness alone can arouse in the human soul. Whenever he approached her, she saw a look of regret on his face. She could never have failed to recognize the demeanor of someone suffering from an ailing conscience. Nor could she have consoled him in the midst of this ailment. For the pangs of conscience are an intractable malady, and the only cure is to disregard them. So disregard them she did, just as she had disregarded—or, at least, pretended to disregard—the sin he had committed against her. Had she not done so, she would not have been able to summon him now to entrust him with her parting guidance.

When she bade him to be seated, he did so with the respectful timidity of a son that had come forth from her very womb. He smiled at her reassuringly, as if in proof that the bond between them—a bond that had grown out of her response to a prophetic inspiration on which she had acted some years before—now ran in his blood and was no longer merely the product of a sacred ritual or charity received.

Her only concern now was to find a point of entry. After circling about him for a time, she said, "I discern a glorious future for you, for the mighty King of the Arabs who dwells in the East will bring you near to him and show you kindness. As for me, like any mother, nothing would make me happier than to be reassured of my children's well-being after I am gone."

She paced around him some more. Then, pausing to look out the window into a naked expanse that was crisscrossed from time to time by flocks of migrating birds, she added, "I am fortunate. In my final days, the Goddess Tanit has granted me an upright son who, after I am gone, will be a benevolent guardian to his two brothers. Tomorrow I will entrust them into your care and send them with you to the army commander Hassan ibn al-Nu'man with the plea that he grant them his favor."

In his eyes she detected a mixture of disapproval and disbelief. Gazing out the window once more at the feathered flocks, she continued, "Everyone who advances in age is destined to pass away, and the same vision that brought me good news about you, brought me good news of my imminent departure. Reaching the road's end means deliverance from the hardships of the journey. How much truer will this be for a seer who has long been awaiting this blessed event?"

As she spoke, she saw him start with alarm. However, determined not to make things easier on him, she said no more.

Suddenly, she heard him ask, "If you expect the imminent battle to bring misfortune, then why don't you cede everything to Ibn al-Nu'man and emigrate? We, as your sons, would be prepared to go with you."

She smiled to herself with pained derision. But she stayed her course.

"You are sons," she replied, "and sons are destined not to depart from this world when their parents do, but to inherit from them. Nevertheless, those who remain on Earth are more to be pitied than those whose time has drawn near. So be courageous. Do not sow the strife that leads to bloodshed. Rather, till the soil for the blissful harvest of peace. Otherwise, you will never find the serenity you were meant to enjoy."

Without another word, she paced the dimly lit chamber like a phantom. Then she paused to say, "In return for my anticipated departure, the Goddess of the Generations has recompensed me with offspring. A mother's survival depends on that of her children, and the Goddess has rewarded me not only once, but twice, since I will be leaving behind a son who, not content merely to inherit my disposition, has merited the power of earthly rule, and will exercise authority over the nations in my stead."

She took a few more steps around the room. Then, leaning forward and giving him a long, thoughtful look, she said in her melodious tongue as though chanting rather than speaking, "*Wattasalid i tamatta tasannan rurim yara ikmaningh ful idyumas amnukal, ayyat ihyayyangh kudid awin ijjisyawad tumasat namanukal!* Have you not heard the story of the mother who, when she was told that her son intended to kill her in order to seize power, replied, 'Let him do so then, if that will enable him to ascend the throne!'"

Narrators have quoted certain mean-spirited individuals as saying that Hassan ibn al-Nu'man had "planted" Khalid ibn Yazid in Dahiya's court, but that Dahiya had outsmarted the emir by turning his would-be intrigue against her into an intrigue against him. In so doing, she had exploited the emir to secure a reign which, if things had gone according to plan, she would have lost at his hands. As for the sages of history, they hold that Dahiya did not plot against her opponent in this ignominious fashion. However, she succeeded in outwitting the Goddess herself, who had robbed her of a reign willed by Fate which—as we have been told by the soothsayers of bygone nations—possesses even greater authority than the gods.

46

The Mission

WHEN HIS ATTENDANTS BROUGHT HIM the happy news that the "the delegation of the impossible" had arrived, he leapt up and left his tent barefoot to see them for himself.

Against a confused chorus of voices outside, Ibn al-Nu'man met alone with Ibn Yazid in the tent. His tone impatient, he asked his old right-hand man, "What's the meaning of this sick joke? Only a genie like Dahiya would do such a thing!"

"You should be happy!" Ibn Yazid responded jovially. "After all, you've recovered a prisoner of war who was lost to you for five years without being asked for anything in return, and with some priceless spoils to boot!"

However, the joke did nothing to satisfy the emir's thirst for revenge. He had been stationed in Barca year after year, laboring to assuage the pangs of defeat while keeping his dreams in check and beseeching those whom the Fates had appointed guardians over the religion to supply him with the soldiers and ammunition he needed to reclaim the umma's lost honor.

Ibn al-Nu'man went on seeking clarification, sometimes directly, other times covertly, unable to conceal the eagerness in his eyes.

At length, taking pity on him, Yazid said, "There is no reason for surprise! Don't the legends speak of her eccentricity?"

"But this isn't eccentricity."

"Call it whatever you like. She insisted on dispatching us to you."

After a pause, he added with a glint of cunning in his eye, "Free of charge!"

"What are you trying to say?" demanded the emir, his gaze burning with curiosity.

Shifting where he sat, Khalid drew a mask over his features before speaking. "She has entrusted her two sons into my care as a good-willed gesture toward you and asks that you treat them well."

There ensued a deep silence interrupted by nothing but the clamor of the soldiers outside.

"Has she decided to surrender?" queried the emir at last.

After an exchange of doubtful glances, Ibn Yazid disappointed the emir at last with a resounding, "No!"

"What does she mean to convey by this gesture, then?"

After a long, piercing glance, Khalid replied, "She wants to die!"

Ibn al-Nu'man looked at Khalid questioningly as if to determine whether he had spoken seriously or in jest. However, he received no reply.

"Die?" he murmured.

Khalid waited briefly before explaining, "She wants to depart this world on the battlefield, not in a peace mediated by capitulation."

"There you have it!" exclaimed the emir. "Another example of the arrogance of polytheism!"

"It isn't arrogance. It's an attempt to escape an ignominy which her people would never agree for her to endure. Her defense of them is also a fulfillment of a duty she has no intention of shirking."

"What harm would it do her to embrace a religion that would protect her in life, and grant her life in death?"

Ibn Yazid gave a cryptic smile. After looking down for a few moments, he explained, "She cannot believe in one religion at the expense of another. In her belief, religions are like the rivers of the world, all of which empty into a single sea which, in the case of religions, is the one God!"

Astonished, the emir asked, "So, does she believe in the one God?"

Looking at the emir intently, Khalid replied, "Not long after my arrival, she asked me to teach her the Quran. She told me that its teachings were no different from what she had inherited from her ancestors in a lost Scripture which they refer to as Anhi."

A smile of derision flickered across Ibn al-Nu'man's lips.

"She was delighted by some verses," Ibn Yazid added.

Then, after a slight hesitation, he continued, "She said that the verse that reads, 'To God belong the East and the West. So whithersoever you turn, there is the face of God,' validates the faith of all those we are accustomed to referring to as 'idol-worshipers.'"

"Oohh!" exclaimed the emir, a pained look on his face. "This is the price we pay for our tolerance toward the likes of Hanash, whose blasphemies precede us wherever we go!"

Silence reigned anew.

Softening somewhat, the emir inquired, "Have your two so-called brothers embraced Islam?"

"Oh yes! I led them in uttering the testimonies of faith."

"So," the emir murmured, "What do you intend to do with them?"

"That's up to the emir," replied Khalid, shooting him a side glance.

The emir said nothing for a time.

Then he announced, "I'll have you lead them out on horseback. But first, they must raise me an army of twelve thousand of their countrymen, six thousand under each one's command, to be a vanguard against their own people!"

47

Wrongdoing

As HE ROAMED THE EXPANSES, Ibn al-Nu'man couldn't help but wonder about the character of this genie who had penned her death certificate with her own hand, then summoned him forthwith to a duel, not in pursuit of victory, but in fulfillment of a duty. The same genie who had insisted on supporting him when he turned tail in flight now insisted on defeating him as he advanced. Yesterday she had supported him by relinquishing to him a precious war prize—the notables of his tribe whom she had taken captive—only to throw down the gauntlet today by affirming her confidence in his character by entrusting him with offspring who, in her culture, were *quruh al-ruh*—wounds to the spirit. In both cases, she had been trusting him to act on his nobler instincts, as though she were testing him to determine whether he was worthy to be her rival. Meanwhile, certain deranged individuals from his camp had the temerity to brand her a polytheist, condemning her as an idol-worshiper, as though the Almighty had appointed them guardians of Truth.

Ibn al-Nu'man had once denied any commonality between himself and this adversary whom he had come not to kill, but to guide to the truth, only to find that she embraced the very values he and other messengers of the conquest had come to advocate. By dismissing such an adversary as a polytheist, he had fallen into the same sin into which his forebears in conquest had fallen. Uqba ibn Nafi's treatment of Kusaila had been clear evidence of the tendency to claim that one alone possesses the truth, and the disregard for others that results from this arrogant mentality. He had forgotten—or pretended to forget—that these nations had not been born yesterday, but had existed on Earth long before he had, and that the Islamic message to which he had devoted himself had been preceded by similar messages whose bearers had led their peoples to faith. In his zeal to spread the literal meaning of his message, he had lost sight of one of its core principles—faith in the validity of earlier messengers and their messages. He had not been sent to evangelize heathen or barbarian nations but simply to remind them of the truth that had been preached by messengers who had come before them.

How could he claim to be pious, even boast of being a lover of God, and accept the majestic title of al-Shaykh al-Amin—the Trustworthy Guide—given him in recognition of his upright life, only to abuse people on the pretext that he had embraced faith in the one and only God first? For all he knew, they might well have embraced the faith before he did, but simply have spoken of it in a different language or in terms of a different culture, all the while preserving its essential core.

How could he, in fairness, order them killed before questioning them concerning their willingness to embrace his religion? How could he condemn them to death before testing them or hearing what they had to say? Was it not their right to reject the religion of a people who had come against them with swords, leaving them no choice but to defend themselves? Had he or others of his faith sent delegations of religious scholars to debate with them and guide them aright before taking up arms against them? By what right did he demand that these people think well of him or of fellow religionists who had reached them before he did, after having seen them make a rush for their share of the spoils?

The entire curse lay in the spoils that had seduced the armies of God. Instead of demonstrating their piety in their treatment of others, they had allowed the spoils of war to become bait for every adventurer with a thirst for riches. The amassment of spoils had become the ultimate purpose of their military expeditions. Africa—now synonymous with enrichment—was preferred by bogus mujahideen over all other destinations. Its wealth had become its curse, turning it into little more than a golden goose for the Muslims' state treasury. Having developed an appetite for the treasures that now flooded into their coffers from this vast continent, the caliphs turned a blind eye to the heinous sins committed against its inhabitants. A similar phenomenon had occurred in relation to the jizya, which was levied not only on Jews and Christians who had clung to their faith of origin, but on people who had publicly proclaimed themselves Muslims.

The crux of the problem lay in the rabble who, when it came to spoils of war, refused to recognize the explicit teachings of Islamic law and who, if their commanders attempted to appeal to the teachings of the religion in this regard, would rise up against them.

When it came to the worship of booty, the rulers themselves were even more egregious than the bogus mujahideen who made up the backbone of the Muslim army. There was collusion from the caliphs, whose insatiable thirst exceeded even that of the rabble. As for Ibn al-Nu'man, he would gladly have leapt to the defense of his religion against these travesties. However, he knew there would be no use in doing so. Caught between these two worldly camps, he had often thought of joining Zubayr's "gang" and sympathizing with the otherworldly Hanash despite his reservations about the latter's verbal excesses. He had voiced these reservations to Hanash himself, hoping to rein in his mystical outbursts. But it was too late for any of that now. All he could do at this stage was to announce publicly that he was relinquishing the title of al-Shaykh al-Amin, not because he had seized a share of booty, taken over a caravan of concubines, or built sumptuous mansions for himself, but because he had failed to speak out against wrongdoing. This alone was surely sufficient reason to divest himself of an honorific he had obtained based on the high regard of virtuous souls whom he had later betrayed.

Wrongdoing and injustice, whether his own or others', had been a thorn in his side ever since he had taken a position of authority, but he had lacked the means to change them by either actions or words. The best he could have done would have been to change it in his heart—an act encouraged by the Seal of the Messengers as the weakest expression of faith.

48

The Imam

SINCE TIME IMMEMORIAL, PEOPLE HAVE decried the disappearance of the living into death. Over time, however, they came to hold the dead sacred and honored them by building tombs even though, logically speaking, the presence of tombs was a natural outcome of the death of those who lay within them. Shrines were built to recognize the virtues of those who had passed away. In some cases, however, the dead were viewed as being absent from their graves, which was taken as evidence that they had been chosen by God and as proof of miraculous powers that qualified them to be severed from the lower world and ushered into the Unseen Realm of the heavens. This was not seen as a final farewell; they would wait there until it was time for them to return to Earth, bringing deliverance with them.

Creation bears witness to the fact that when the religions on which people have relied so wholeheartedly disappoint their hopes through their failure to root out injustice and bring the promised Paradise to Earth, they strain to take matters into their own hands. When this happens, the body of the deceased acquires mythical wings on which it soars aloft, then dwells in the heavenly kingdom for a time. Its presence in the divine sanctuary gives it a special place in the psyche of some messenger on Earth, though of course doubters disbelieve the messenger because he is a mortal like them. However, when the message fails to achieve the justice to which virtuous souls aspire, their distrust persists even if the mission to spread the message is triumphant. The prophecy is quick to be exiled along with the seeker who has borne its burden. As a result, confusion reigns once more on Earth, and the weak and oppressed are forced to seek refuge in their age-old opium: the dream of resurrection!

Resurrection—the revival of the spirit in a religion deadened by the worship of its literal message—can only be achieved by a miracle, a ransom, a sacrifice that purges creatures of their earthly disposition and negates their mortality. By virtue of their presence in the expanses of the Lost Dimension and by the grace of the Deity's inimitable power, such creatures take on attributes of the Divine. Seekers have referred metaphorically to such a heavenly figure as al-Muntazar, "the Awaited." By virtue of his occultation, Jesus was freed from his earthly essence, thus becoming al-Muntazar. Similarly, Muhammad shed his worldly identity in the Mi'raj, or heavenly ascent, and was transformed by the law of the dream into al-Mahdi al-Muntazar, "the Rightly Guided and Awaited."

Dahiya the Seer, Soothsayer of the Generations, was likewise transported from a realm in which the *adhan*, or Muslim call to prayer, was sounded, and whose inhabitants had embraced Islam, to the selfsame lost dimension where—like all bearers of the good news of salvation—she took on the qualities of a savior and became al-Imam al-Muntazar, "the Awaited Imam." According to the teachings of the Ibadi sect, Dahiya will return one day from her occultation to her namesake city of Tahert ("the Lioness"), where she will deliver the umma from captivity and lead believers in the Friday communal prayer which has been postponed due to her absence. The day once known as Friday will then be understood to be a metaphor for the Day of Promise—the day that will bring salvation to all the world's weak and oppressed.

As the old poet of Thouda so loved to chant as he made his rounds among the tribes, they had converted to Islam—they had embraced faith. However, the faith in their hearts had remained an empty sanctuary, embodied in a mosque teeming with worshipers who, rather than praying, awaited the arrival of their lost imam to lead them. They had no choice but to wait for the coming of the one whom the Deity had chosen not merely as someone whom the Divine addresses from behind a veil, but as His beloved.

The dream that Dahiya would one day appear miraculously in their prayer niche persisted even during the upheavals that afflicted the religion in later historical periods. Such upheavals shook the faith of those thirsty for God and split the umma into factions that fought mercilessly among themselves, each of them claiming to possess the true understanding of the religion. The faction that emerged under Dahiya's reign came to be known as the Ibadi sect, whose doctrines and rites only strengthened their faith in the day when their beloved Seer would be restored from her exile. Dwelling among them as a ferocious she-lion, she would lead the faithful in the Friday prayer that had been postponed for so long in anticipation of her promised return and reclamation of her erstwhile role as mediator with the Deity.

Humanity's age-old thirst for God has endured down the millennia, reaching its pinnacle during the Middle Ages, when the choicest members of this umma first established the divinely ordained entity referred to in history books as the *ribat*—a place where Sufi mystics would seek solitude with God. Over time, this solitude took the form of a covenant with God that found expression in a legendary empire known as the Almoravid State, which extended from Barca in the East to the expanses of Andalusia in the West.

49

Woe

"You're the one at fault! You shouldn't have brought daughters into the world!"

These are the words others would fling in his face whenever he expressed his bitterness toward the foreigners. They might as well have been flinging stones at him like some stray dog.

Then they would continue on their way without waiting for his reply: "And do we have the power to choose whether we father males or females?"

One of these rogues replied in turn, saying, "If the Fates had granted you a male, you would have even more regrets. For while a female may be destined to be kidnapped and sold in the foreigners' markets as a prostitute, the fate of sons is to be killed!"

Then he erupted in an odious cackle before taking his leave.

As for the emir's chamberlain, he attempted to console him, saying, "I understand your distress. However, you should know that you are not alone. Whenever wars break out, women are their first victims, and most households have lost their daughters. When injustice afflicts one and all, it has traditionally been viewed as a kind of 'justice'!"

The bereaved father continued to make the rounds of the tribes, hovering about the commanders of the invading army and begging for a means of recovering his lost treasure. In the course of this feverish quest, he nearly wasted away, his body the bearer of his tribulation.

When he asked why such misfortune had befallen him, he was simply told that woe is the curse of all who are defeated in war. Still burning with questions, he asked why he should be defeated when he had so heroically defended his womenfolk. Here he was told that the secret lay in religion: generation after generation has attested to the impossibility of losing a war waged in the name of a religion because of the invincibility of faith.

Still, he wondered: Isn't defense of one's honor and womenfolk also a form of religion? Indeed, the drive to defend one's honor is sometimes a force more powerful than religion itself. As he pondered this truth in the course of his mad circuit, he encountered a passerby from his community who revealed to him another aspect of the conundrum. The astute wayfarer drew him in with a passing question about his relationship with his neighbor, but when he was about to answer, the words caught in his throat.

"Do you see?" said the wayfarer. "You hesitate because you are ashamed, and you are ashamed because you do not want to admit that you have never trusted a neighbor. Moreover, what is said about neighbors can also be said of relatives, what is said about a relative can be said about the clan, what is said about the clan can be said about the tribe, and what is said about a tribe can be said about the nation. How can a nation whose members profess the religion of hatred ever aspire to victory? On the contrary, a nation in the grip of hatred will defeat itself even before it enters the battlefield. It will end up a feast on the table of any foe who approaches even with an army of ghosts. How much more defenseless will it be in the face of a mighty army driven by the most powerful rationale in the world—religion?"

As he reflected on the wisdom proffered by this unknown sage, he began searching himself, delving into his memory and examining his actions over years past. What he discovered was that what the stranger had referred to as hatred had been a malady in his own life. Indeed, it had run in his blood, poisoning his relationships with cynicism and distrust. But when he attempted to lift himself out of its depths, he found to his dismay that his entire life had been nothing but a nightmare in which everyone was pitted against everyone else, and that had he not fled into seclusion, he would not have survived the intrigues of his own kin. How could he have trusted his neighbor or clan? The lost Scripture had warned against succumbing to the scourge of hatred, which was bound to lead to the annihilation of the community. Yet he, like so many others, had disregarded this teaching.

And the reason? The reason, as the stranger explained to him, was that people had made light of the Scripture, which would never have come to be described as "lost" if those who inherited it had not paid it proud lip service without preserving it in their hearts. It was no longer evident in their conduct, and their present lost state was the consequence. For the law set forth in the commandments becomes a refuge when it is translated into action. However, if it lingers too long on a poisoned organ like the tongue, it grows weak and corrupt.

As for the invaders, they had been powerful enough to wrest his offspring away from him because the Scripture whose message they had come to spread was still alive in their hearts and not just a mere morsel in their mouths. He had had no consolation to offer his wife, who wailed at the top of her lungs, "Woe is me! Woe is me! I have lost in my lifetime what was to preserve me after my death!"

Yet wailing did nothing to quench the fire in her bosom, and after losing hope of recovering her daughters, she breathed her last. Like her husband, she had reached the age of fifty, at which point any loss she endured would be irreparable.

The only means he now had of alleviating his affliction would be to acquire enough silver and gold to be able to join his three lost daughters in their place of exile, hoping against hope that by following the counsel he had received from a certain man of virtue and wisdom, he might find them at last.

50

Peace

AFTER HIT-AND-RUN CAMPAIGNS that went on for years, the entire West had at last granted him its allegiance. The time had come for him to rest. But had this rest yielded him any satisfaction?

As he sat ensconced in his abode, Ibn al-Nuʻman gave a disdainful smile. The rest he had so hoped for throughout his struggle with his fate was not the kind of rest envisaged by the foolish when they anticipate the prize they call "victory." Only they who have experienced loss understand that it is precisely in this odious outcome that the longed-for rest is to be found! As for victory, it has nothing to offer but confusion!

Throughout the years of his brokenness in the face of the Genie's might, he had experienced a peace of mind that had enabled him to defy his fate. This is what he had been doing when he chose to make his home in Barca, erecting edifices of stone. By means of these edifices, he had bestowed honor on a site which for generations had been viewed as a mere crossing—a bridge of sorts—connecting East to West. Indeed, it had derived its name from certain spiteful folks who had referred to it disparagingly as "a road."

It was here that, after his setback, Ibn Nuʻman had gone to be alone, to search for himself within himself far from the ruckus created by illusions and their deceit. Otherwise, he couldn't have nursed his wounds, then gone on to spend years building a city—not simply to pass the time, as ignorant souls might have surmised, but to defy his loss by transforming it into a gain through a building project of a sort that invaders before him had had no interest in.

Furthermore, he had raised these edifices in an impossible location—a low-lying salt marsh that would not have been expected to bear their weight. Of course, none of this would have transpired had it not been for the wounds he had suffered, and the defeat in which weak souls would have seen nothing but a kind of death. Yet he had learned how to make good use of others' perceptions of him, knowing that the defeated party—which he had been at the time—would be viewed by everyone else, the caliph included, as exempt from all expectations. After all, he had lost everything. It was sufficient that he was wounded and ill. Indeed, he had been counted among the dead! The dead alone can seclude themselves, since to others they have no existence, and he alone who has no existence can be at peace with himself, since nothing is demanded of him.

Ibn al-Nu'man had consoled himself in the beginning with the thought that supplies and reinforcements would be arriving from the East. Given the caliph's long-standing preoccupation with his war against Abdullah ibn al-Zubayr, he held out little hope of receiving them. After lengthy reflection, he had decided to seek out an unlikely dream. Heeding an importunate inner summons, he had set out on an intrepid mount that would blaze a trail to the heavens. The heights are always a dream and the path leading to them is the challenge. This "intrepid mount" would consist of stones of the sort that had enchanted him since childhood, when everything else around him had appeared fragile and delicate by comparison. These structures would mock death and annihilation!

Even though Ibn al-Nu'man himself was skeptical of immortality, he sought refuge in these stones, not in pursuit of some glory which his opponents—and he himself—might have expected to indwell the resulting monuments. Rather, he did it to appease an obsession which, questionable though it was, was so insistent that it had established a presence for itself in his mind and heart. In one sense, he may have succeeded in having his say through these monuments, whose hard stones had been extracted from Earth's proud strongholds and to which others referred admiringly as "Hassan's palaces." In another sense, however, he realized that he had failed. Perhaps he had misinterpreted the dream, led astray by his own perceptions. Despite their epic beauty and impregnability, and the promise that dwells in the heights, these stones had not brought him a single step closer to the Divine.

Had he hoped to compensate for his failure to achieve victory for God with his sword by resorting to stones which, he hoped, would grant him a firm hold on the divine benefaction? Even the elegant mosque that stood in the center of his ring of mansions had failed to intercede on his behalf, just as his predecessor, Ibn Nafi, had failed to build Kairouan, whose grand mosque had not cleansed him of the sins he had committed against innocents who had bled, and continued to bleed, on his account.

Perhaps he needed to recognize that the nearness of God was conditional upon the mercy one had shown to one's fellow human beings, that the love of God consisted in ceasing to shed innocent blood, and that if the shedding of innocent blood was the condition for filling the Muslims' state treasury, it would be better for its springs to run dry. No mosque could intercede for him, nor could any edifice purchase divine approval. His deliverance lay in one path: ceasing to kill and making pilgrimage to the only house of God that could guarantee inner tranquility—the pursuit of peace!

Stepping out of his pavilion, he went wandering through the open spaces as was his custom whenever he sought a solution to a conundrum or a way out of a dilemma. He surrendered the reins to the magnanimous void, which had never once failed him, and which had always been a healing balm in his isolation. Following his recent victory, he had feared the worst, knowing that while people might forgive defeat, they would never forgive victory. The calm that had followed the conquest did not bode well in the East, where foes lay in wait. For wherever foes lie in wait, a plot is in the making.

Those who have transcended the ephemeralities of this world, placing themselves entirely at God's disposal, need regret nothing. His only concern now was to address the caliph. He wanted to announce the glad tidings that, now that he had defeated al-Kahina and reached an amicable agreement with the non-Muslims over the jizya, peace had returned to Africa.

51

The Successor

"I HAVE GOOD NEWS FOR you!" exclaimed Ibn al-Nu'man as soon as Khalid ibn Yazid appeared before him. Cradling the leather scroll in his hand as though it were a gold ingot whose weight he was gauging, he added, "I'm delighted for two reasons: firstly, because the governorship has sought you out during my reign, and secondly, because the decree regarding the governorship bears the seal of the caliph himself, not his brother Abd al-Aziz!"

Ibn Yazid cracked a curious smile as the emir continued, "The prestige you gain here derives not from your being appointed governor over Tripoli but rather, from the fact that the appointment was made by the caliph himself!"

The curiosity that had been etched on Ibn Yazid's features faded into a look of ambivalence.

The emir continued, "Only those who know what a sly fox Abd al-Malik is would be able to discern his true motive here. As I see it, he has bestowed this honor upon you to reward you for your outstanding performance during the years of your captivity in Dahiya's territory."

The look of ambivalence on Ibn Yazid's face now turned to one of scorn. Shifting uneasily in his seat, he mumbled, "Would that it had indeed been captivity!"

"In our book, it *was* captivity," insisted the emir. "It's simply that it was captivity with good treatment. And if it weren't for what you so cleverly concealed inside a loaf of bread, we would not have been able to assess al-Kahina's situation, nor would we have risked an advance on her despite the arrival of the reinforcements."

The emir paused for a moment and leaned toward his guest. Then, clutching the precious parchment close to his chest and resisting a boyish mischievousness that gleamed in his eyes, he whispered as though divulging a secret, "And despite the fact that half its contents had gone up in smoke!"

Flinging his head back, Ibn al-Nu'man shook with muffled laughter before recovering his dignified bearing.

"As a matter of fact, your invitation to break camp was sufficient indication of what had happened in al-Kahina's territory. After recalling the ruin she had brought upon her realm through her own folly, it wasn't difficult to guess what the situation was. All in all, then, credit for our victory goes to that trick of yours!"

However, Ibn Yazid's response to the emir's praise came as a disappointment. "Yet despite it all," he replied, "she didn't fall for the trick. If it hadn't been for her tolerance, I would have paid for that boyish prank with my life!"

"Don't disparage an action that was a cause of victory, even if it appeared to be a boyish stunt. Who knows? This child-like spirit of yours may be what protected you from a violent response on her part!"

Ibn Yazid's features clouded over and his voice took on a different tone.

"On the contrary," he objected, "what protected me was the mother in her, the mother I've now betrayed. If she didn't truly see me as her son, she wouldn't have forgiven me for what I did!"

Gazing at him curiously, Ibn al-Nu'man asked, "Do you really think she would forgive the son she had gained through that ridiculous rite of kinship for a betrayal as great as this one?"

Stiffening, Ibn Yazid said, "Why wouldn't she? Don't we also believe in the power of mother's milk to form a binding covenant? If it weren't for this belief, Abdullah ibn Abi Sarh would not have escaped death, as it was his milk-brother, Uthman ibn Affan, who interceded on his behalf to deliver him from a death sentence that had been handed down against him by the Seal of the Prophets himself."

The emir fell silent. The two men exchanged a glance.

Ibn Yazid added, "Not only did she forgive me for my transgression, but she predicted the honor I would receive."

The emir sought clarification with a cock of the head. When his guest made no reply, he resorted to words.

"Really?" he asked.

"She told me I would attain great stature under the mighty monarch who dwells in the East."

"Astrologers lie even if they speak the truth," muttered the emir absently.

"But she spoke the truth, and I didn't believe her!" argued Ibn Yazid.

The emir said nothing.

"Besides," Ibn Yazid added, "this governorship isn't an acknowledgment of heroism. It's a reward for treason!"

Shaking his finger ominously, his face somber, the emir retorted, "If I were you, I wouldn't think that way. Watch out!"

Nevertheless, Ibn Yazid ventured into a lost dimension, saying, "She suckled me on a tenderness and affection I never received from my birth mother!"

"Be careful with your words!" cried the emir.

Ibn Yazid pressed onward through the lost realm. "She used to dream of all the nations of the world becoming brothers. She conceived a son by a foreigner so that he could be a brother to the son she had borne to a fellow countryman. It was a cause of great distress to her that she hadn't been able to suckle me at her breast, since long before I came to her, her milk had gone dry."

Choking on a lump in his throat, Ibn Yazid spit out a statement which, welling up out of the unexplored regions of the spirit, was as bitter as it was brief: "She loved me!"

"You mustn't forget," the emir cried, "that you're more her son now than you were yesterday! And when you assume the governorship, you will do so as the offspring of a queen known as Dahiya. Perhaps you remember the well-known story about the queen mother who, when informed that her son intended to kill her and usurp the throne, responded with the words, 'Let him do so, then! The important thing is that he rule!' A mother will be prepared to sacrifice herself for the sake of ensuring that her son rises to prominence after her, even at the cost of her own life!"

Panting with agitation, the emir fell silent. After catching his breath, he resumed, "She has forgiven you for your sins against her because she knows that her reign will continue through you, since you are her son!"

Drawing in another breath, he added, "If she had responded in any other way, she would not be worthy of the title Dahiya—the Cunning One."

When, after a pause, Ibn al-Nu'man glimpsed a large tear escaping from his companion's eye, he murmured, "Don't forget that you're her successor now!"

As if he were thinking aloud, Ibn Yazid said, "It wasn't we who defeated her. She defeated herself. She decided to step aside and deliver us a victory which, thanks to her, we have now won at no cost to us!"

52

The Renunciation

SEVERAL DAYS LATER, IBN AL-NUʿMAN was spending time alone in the open desert near his camp in Kairouan. By this time, Tripoli and its environs had been removed from his jurisdiction, leaving him with the region of Kairouan and the region beyond it. The opponents who had taken these measures believed that this new division would spoil his happiness over his defeat of al-Kahina. Little did these riffraff know that his delight over seeing peace restored was greater than any he could have experienced over a military victory. They were certain not to be content with this insult—or what they deemed to have been an insult—but would hatch still more plots against him. The removal of Tripoli from his sphere of influence had been just the beginning, since Abd al-Aziz ibn Marwan would do everything in his power to ensure that Ibn al-Nuʿman paid dearly for a victory he had won with reinforcements received directly from the caliph rather than through Abd al-Aziz's mediation.

Indeed, news emerging from Fustat indicated that Abd al-Aziz was resentful over the spoils' delayed arrival and enraged over what he deemed to be his puny portion in comparison with the lion's share pouring into the coffers of the state treasury in Damascus. Did this mean that Ibn al-Nuʿman should expect the worst? What, of all the fates Abd al-Aziz might have planned for him, could have been worse than stripping him of the governorship? However, Abd al-Aziz seemed not to realize that the governorship which he personally viewed as a kind of paradise was for Ibn al-Nuʻman on the order of a punishment, and that being stripped of it, far from being a punishment, would be a form of deliverance.

The disc of the sun knelt on the Western horizon, inundating the visible expanse with a bloody deluge that promised a stifling day on the morrow. Ibn al-Nuʻman's return to the city coincided with the descent of dusk and the arrival of a scout from the East. He watched the scout who, as he had seen him do on frequent occasions, joked with the patrols at the gate. A short distance later, he stopped to speak with the herald while still mounted on his horse.

The scout is as indispensable to an army as the herald is to the walled-in life of a city. The former reveals what has been concealed beyond the walls, while the latter gives voice to the ever-changing realities within them. These two figures are abiding phantoms, ever faithful to their roles as they answer the ever-repeating summons of the night in its eternal bargain with the day. So long as the day vanishes into the dark of night, and the night is obliterated by the light of day, the covenant between them will endure.

Ibn al-Nuʻman smiled as he heard the herald call out, "Does the day come bearing good news in its quiver, or bad?"

The scout leaned forward on his mount to speak to the herald as though he were about to confide a secret.

"It isn't for me to judge what's in the quiver," he remarked. "After all, the Realm of the Unseen can turn what we had thought to be good news into bad and what we had taken to be bad news into good."

The herald, voicing his agreement with the scout, clutched the horse's bridle lest the horseman escape before he got what he was after.

"You speak truly!" he concurred. "Reports are our daily nourishment, though we fear what a report may contain, knowing that it may concern new masters whom the Fates have granted power over us in place of others!"

Leaning forward a few inches more, the horseman queried, "What would I gain were I to satisfy the herald's curiosity?"

"Satisfy my curiosity!" exclaimed the herald. "Nothing could do that this side of the grave. Death alone will bring the ear's longings to an end."

"In any case," declared the horseman after some hesitation, "you'd be well advised to sharpen the weapon you conceal between your jaws, for the new governor is on his way to you!"

Muffling a groan, the herald inquired, "Is this a mere rumor going around among the soldiers, or is it a fact confirmed by a sealed decree?"

The horseman chuckled. "It is a fact confirmed by a sealed decree!"

With that, he prodded his horse and rode away, while the herald stole about among the guards like a ghost.

From his position as spectator, Ibn al-Nu'man stood for a few moments marveling over how just hours earlier his intuition had told him that events would transpire in precisely this way. From that night onward, news would pass from tongue to tongue until at the appointed time the messenger arrived to place the awaited decree in his hands.

Umayyad governors were constant victims of the machinations of Abd al-Malik and his brothers, in whose hands they were mere pawns rather than rulers in the true sense of the word. Abd al-Aziz sought retribution against Ibn al-Nu'man for having gone over his head by requesting reinforcements directly from the caliph. In addition to removing him from his post, Abd al-Aziz planned to seize all the spoils Ibn al-Nu'man would bring with him on his way to Damascus. He intended to strip him of every last item of value so that he would reach the caliph empty handed.

As for Ibn al-Nu'man, he planned to teach Abd al-Aziz a lesson. He would turn the tables on him! The roguish Abd al-Aziz knew very well that there was no way to reach

Damascus from North Africa without passing through Fustat, where he was stationed as Governor of Egypt. He also knew that spoils were not something one could easily keep out of sight. But what this fox didn't know was that he and those of his ilk weren't the only ones with tricks up their sleeves. When he passed through Fustat, Ibn al-Nu'man would conceal items that were lightweight yet precious in ways that Abd al-Aziz would never have dreamed of!

That very night, he would issue instructions for extra water skins to be prepared. He would then have them stuffed full of jewels, gold and silver, which would enable him to smuggle them past Abd al-Aziz and deliver them safely to the seat of the caliphate in Damascus. This accomplished, he would be awarded as many concubines as he could possibly desire. Once the caliph saw the treasures that had arrived hidden in water skins, he would be furious with his brother for removing Ibn al-Nu'man. He would thereupon attempt to reinstate Ibn al-Nu'man by appointing him anew to the governorship from which Abd al-Aziz had so unceremoniously dismissed him. But his attempt would meet with failure! For never again would Ibn al-Nu'man agree to serve as a governor for Banu Umayya. Indeed, never again would he agree to serve as a governor for anyone, since he now knew that a governorship was not truly a governorship—however it might seem to others—but rather, a decree of unofficial slavery!

That's right—he would renounce the post. He would withdraw. He would be liberated. He would find rest in humility. And in his rest, he would suffer no lack of friends or supporters so long as there remained in the world the likes of Hanash Sanaani!

53

The Deadly Diversion
AH 99/721 CE

SIXTEEN YEARS HAD PASSED, DURING which time everything had changed and nothing had changed. Governors had disappeared, to be succeeded by others. People had rejoiced at the departure of one governor, only to sigh over his loss as they found themselves suffering even more badly under his successor. Bound as it is to yield a situation worse than the one that preceded it, the dream we call "change" always brings disappointment in its wake. Even so, human nature would win the day time and time again. No one stopped longing for change, hoping instead for a miracle that would bring the good that seemed never to come.

Nevertheless, people could only express their gratitude to heaven, because the night had not ceased its orbit around the day, nor the day around the night. The Final Judgment had yet to come, as evidenced by the presence of the herald, who hovered about the ruins announcing whatever tidings he had received from the scout, foretelling one governor's departure and another's arrival or the approach of an invader who would take the place of another. Through his presence, the herald provided evidence that they were alive and that anything other than this ever-repeating diversion was an illusion.

By the unanimous agreement of the wise and knowing, it was indeed a diversion. However, it was a deadly diversion, for at the height of this vain struggle, bloodshed had so exceeded its bounds that Earth pled for mercy, while heaven's conscience shed ominous, blood-red rain the likes of which no one had ever seen.

Had the descendants of flesh and blood at last had their fill of bloodshed and its nonsense? Of course not! The hunger for more remained an infernal blaze. Musa ibn Nusayr, the Umayyad general who succeeded Ibn al-Nu'man, prefaced his arrival in Kairouan with a raid on the fortress in Zaghwan a day's journey away where, according to the historian Ibn Idhari, he abused the population, taking female captives numbering in the tens of thousands. Following this, he sent a son by the name of Abdullah into the African interior to bring back still more female captives numbering one hundred thousand (again according to Ibn Idhari). He is then reported to have dispatched his son Marwan, who brought back an equal number again, so that one-fifth of the booty alone came to sixty thousand female captives, the most astronomical number ever reported by those who chronicled the history of the Muslim conquests. Indeed, the caliph is said nearly to have fainted at the news, incredulous that this much booty could possibly have been seized in the course of a single campaign.

According to Ibn Qutayba, Musa ibn Nusayr conquered the region of Sajumat and killed its kings. Not content with this conquest, he then ordered the sons of Uqba ibn Nafi— Ayyad, Uthman, and Abu Ubayda—to avenge their father's death, whereupon they slit the throats of six hundred of the people's notables. As for the figures associated with subsequent campaigns of conquest, they bear witness to an unparalleled appetite for blood. It was as though the entire unfortunate continent of Africa had been reduced to a source of plunder over which the governors vied through murder. The more one murdered, the greater one's share of the spoils and one's favor with the caliphs.

It was only to be expected that during the decade and a half following Ibn al-Nu'man's removal from the governorate, the bitterness and rage of those who had embraced

Islam in response to the Muslim conquests reached their boiling point. The act of converting had done nothing to free them from the burden of the jizya which, according to Islamic law, was only to be levied on Jews and Christians who had chosen to cling to their faith of origin but which, despite this Islamic legal stricture, was being extracted by Umayyad governors from as many people as possible as a means of pillaging their wealth. Those who were unable to pay saw their daughters carried away by force in caravans to the East, where they were sold in the slave markets. The proceeds were used to enrich the Muslims' state treasury and finance the caliphs' profligate lifestyles.

Meantime, a certain desolate, gaunt father with gnarled, rough fingers resembling the claws of a wild animal wandered aimlessly among the tribes. He had been betrayed by the succession of night and day which, not content to streak his hair with gray, had stripped him of every last hair on his head. Despite it all, he had not surrendered to his fate. Rather, he had continued as a wayfarer, feverishly searching for a way to recover his daughters—the wounds to his spirit, as he always referred to his children. Children are their parents' profoundest bliss. Despite the pain that a wound inevitably brings, these are wounds one can't do without and without which existence has no meaning, for they alone are the guarantee of immortality!

And now deliverance was in the offing. Approaching on the backs of caravans, it had been snatched up by the scout, who stood ready to pass it on to others as a prophecy on the lips of the herald who, for his part, would spread it abroad as glad tidings for the oppressed. For in the midst of the deadly diversion, an earthquake had struck, and a new messenger had taken up residence in the seat of the caliphate. He was a messenger intent upon recovering the truth from its distant realm, restoring it to the land of the caliphate, and shoring up the pillars of a long-lost vision—justice!

An elusive entity, justice had over the course of the generations become little more than a dream, and since the time when prophets and apostles had ceased to appear, most people had despaired of finding it. Indeed, in the absence of justice, the earth had ceased to recognize herself.

Now, however, people East and West called out to one another. The news was spread abroad by the oppressed throughout the lands where the call to prayer was sounded, repeating the name: "Umar ibn Abd al-Aziz"!

54

Lying

THE NAME UMAR IBN ABD al-Aziz rolled off people's tongues like a magic spell. But how was one to reach the fortress where the source of this magic made his dwelling?

Tribal elders came from all over to select a delegation that would journey to the legendary East, where they would seek deliverance from the man whom heaven had placed in its service on Earth, there to establish justice in a land plagued with falsehood.

Coming from Zaghwan, Hawwara, Sijilmasa, Garamante, Sujuma, Tahert, Thouda, Nafusa, Tangiers, the Land of al-Sus, Butur territory, Masmuda, Zanata, Mighrawa, and other parts which until recently had been unknown, they gathered in Kairouan. They debated among themselves for three days without reaching agreement. The inability to agree on a single point of view had been their point of weakness for as long as anyone could remember. Over time, it had become a malignant tumor that threatened their very existence. Not content simply to drive wedges into their alliances, this spirit of contention had awakened hatred and enmity among them to the point of bloodshed.

It is said that the roots of this malady went back to a distant era in which their ancestors had been visited by a sage from the East whom certain foolish souls had denied the proper hospitality. As a result, he had grown bitter toward the entire community and had sworn to afflict it with an ailment

239

for which it could find no cure. As the story goes, this sage devised a deadly amulet which he deposited inside the hide of a piebald dog. He then hid it deep inside a remote cave. Thereafter, the tribes began to notice that whenever they met to consult about a matter, they would come away even more bent on division than they had been before, and from that time onward they had never once agreed on anything.

On this occasion, as usual, they disagreed. First they disagreed over who the members of the delegation should be. Then, rather than waiting until they had finished discussing this point, they moved on suddenly to another topic of even more critical importance: who would head the delegation. Failure to agree on this point would have rendered the entire gathering of no effect, and all on account of a deadly amulet planted by the sage in the hide of a piebald dog! Had it not been for the intervention of certain prudent individuals, the gathering would have ended in disaster.

The third item on the agenda, which sparked the most vehement altercation of all, was the question of how to reach the place where they hoped to find deliverance. Some of those gathered felt it would be too dangerous to take the coastal road to Egypt, since, as soon as the governors' spies learned of their intentions, they were sure to intercept them and send them back to where they had come from. At this point, a sharp debate erupted when one of them, his patience worn thin, jumped to his feet and shouted at the top of his lungs, "Are you asking us to violate our law by lying about our intentions just as we are on our way to the place where we hope to recover our true dignity?"

A heated discussion ensued over the matter of inward intention. One group argued that it was permissible to lie if the purpose of the lie was to defend the truth, whereas others condemned this stance. True, they said, if they had indulged in a wicked vice like that of lying, they would not have lost a single war with the Arabs, and they would not have lost their

240

state or their children, on whose account they were now gathering in the hope of finding a way to recover them. However, they would have forfeited their honor!

In the end, they had no choice but to adopt a compromise solution, which was to divide the delegation into two groups. One group would pass through Fustat on its way to the Hijaz to perform the rites of pilgrimage to Mecca, after which it would go by caravan to the seat of the caliphate in Damascus. This plan was designed to appease the consciences of those who disapproved of lying concerning the delegation's intended destination. As for the second group, consisting of those who did not view it as a sin to conceal their intentions, they would pass through Fustat with the tribes heading directly for Damascus.

Once they had adopted this solution, they found it easier to resolve the second point, namely, who should head the delegation. The choice of a head for the delegation worked like magic in facilitating the selection of the delegation members, one of whom was a certain gaunt elder who had virtually wasted away with grief, becoming little more than a ghost, and whose selection brought the painful ordeal to a close.

55

The Greater River

Damascus, the Caliphal Palace, AH 100/722 CE

"MUHAMMAD DID NOT COME TO our world as a tax collector.
He came as a guide!"

After repeating the statement twice in the presence of the
foreign delegation, the caliph fell silent.

He contemplated the pilgrims who had come from the
distant lands in the West, his features graced with a tran-
quil expression that bespoke an intimate warmth. His guests
whispered among themselves, laboring to translate into their
respective tongues the meaning of a certain word—*sakina*, or
divinely inspired peace of mind—of which religious scholars
had spoken so often when they had come to teach them the
rites of Islamic worship, and which the caliph's genteel manner
brought to mind. They were charmed by the air of kindness
this man exuded, a kindness they had not been accustomed
to encountering in the demeanor of governors, army commanders, or soldiers who were constantly pursing their lips
and were invariably gloomy and condescending. They knew
they were in the presence of an apostle.

When the Umayyads were at last overtaken by the sword
of justice, Umar ibn Abd al-Aziz wrested from them what they
had wrested unjustly from the Muslim community. The Umayyads then sought out Fatima bint Marwan (Umar's paternal
aunt) for protection, asking her to intercede on their behalf. As
we read in the annals of Islamic history, Umar addressed his
paternal aunt with the words:

God Almighty, blessed be He, sent Muhammad, may God's blessings and peace be upon him, not as a chastisement, but as a source of mercy to all people. Then He took him unto Himself, having chosen to bring him into His own presence. Upon his death, Muhammad left a river from which all of his people were to drink equally. He was succeeded by Abu Bakr, who left the river as it was. Abu Bakr was succeeded by Umar, who emulated his companion and predecessor. However, when Uthman came, he derived a second river from the first. Uthman was followed by Muawiya, who split the river into numerous rivers. The river then went on dividing with Yazid, Marwan, Abd al-Malik, al-Walid, and Sulayman, and on down to me. The greater river has now dried up, and its owners will not be given to drink from it until it is restored for them to what it was before.

According to Muslim historians, including Abu-l-Faraj al-Isfahani, author of *Kitab al-aghani*, Fatima bint Marwan then returned to her house surrounded by the chiefs of Banu Umayya, who were incredulous over what had befallen them, and said simply, "Taste the bitter fruit of having married into the family of Umar ibn al-Khattab!" (Umar ibn al-Khattab, the legendary caliph known for crowning faith with justice, was the maternal grandfather of Umar ibn Abd al-Aziz.)

It is said that when he received the delegation from the land of the non-Arabs in pursuit of justice, the Commander of the Faithful made the same statement with which he had addressed the Umayyads on the day he became caliph. After repeating these words to the delegation visiting from the Greater Maghreb, the caliph added that he would instruct the judiciary to issue a fatwa on their case. He pledged to release them from the burden of the unjust jizya, and to resolve the matter of their missing children, who, if still alive, would be brought back accompanied by their own children, even if they had been fathered by an Umayyad governor. He also promised to pay adequate compensation for the damages caused by the deaths of those whom Fate had snatched away before their time. Upon hearing these things, the members of the delegation cheered the illustrious emir as though they had won a victory on the battlefield, praising the Almighty in a chorus of many languages.

Still, would those who had developed a taste for ill-gotten spoils accept such a defeat, even if it had come in the form of an order handed down by the highest authority in the land?

56

The Recitation

FACED WITH THE DISASTER THAT had befallen them so suddenly and for which they had been so entirely unprepared, it was now the Umayyads' turn to gather. In this respect they were like anyone who, having grown accustomed to a life of comfort and ease, wakes up one day to find that their comfort and ease have given way to misery and hardship.

True to his word, the caliph had ordered that those who had enjoyed status and favor be stripped of their illicit gain, concubines included, and that everything be restored to its proper place. In addition, he had appointed over Africa the man who came to be known in the annals of history as the best of governors to serve under the best of caliphs, Ismail ibn Abi al-Muhajir, who brought the inhabitants of North Africa into Islam through kindness and persuasion rather than by the sword. Ismail ibn Abi al-Muhajir taught people the basic rites and duties of Islam. He also taught them how to distinguish between halal and haram, the permissible and the forbidden, without which religious rites would be devoid of meaning. In order to carry out these tasks, the governor called upon a group of the finest Successors to the Companions of the Prophet, including Abd al-Rahman ibn Nafi and Saad ibn Mas'ud al-Nujaybi.

The discredited Umayyads came together in one forum after another until, at last, they concluded that it would be necessary to form a delegation to meet with the caliph in the hope that he might lighten the burden on the notables who, restless and discontent, would not remain silent for long unless the situation was redressed, and unless the caliph could be persuaded to reverse his decision before it was too late.

In the course of their deliberations, the Umayyads were advised by a certain sly old fox among them to seek assistance from the treasurer, a fellow conniver whom Umar ibn Abd al-Aziz had "inherited" from his predecessor, Sulayman ibn Abd al-Malik. Accordingly, they sought out the treasurer, hoping he might persuade the caliph of what would befall the State Treasury if the inhabitants of Africa were relieved of the jizya. In fact, the man came readily to their aid, armed with all the expertise at his disposal on the delicate and ignoble topic of money. In his forties, the treasurer was a man of slight build whose rectangular face bore a suspicious-looking expression that seemed to conceal some vague, perpetual discontent, and whose conical beard ended in wisps, like a broomstick bared of its bristles by the passage of time. He wore a brocade turban borrowed from the attire native to Bukhara or Khazaria, from whose people he was said to be descended.

The first thing this sprite did was to choose two men of Banu Umayya who were known for their shrewdness and cunning. He declined to involve any others in the mission; his rationale was that if the delegation consisted of more than three members, their logic would be less cogent, or they might say more than they ought to and lose their persuasive power. The discussion would then dissolve into little more than a shouting match, and the mission would fail.

The villain then lay in wait for the caliph, while his accomplices ensured that he was surrounded by myrmidons who would bring reports on the caliph's comings and goings. The most important thing, however, was to monitor his mood, which was the greatest obstacle they faced. After ascending the throne of the caliphate, Umar ibn Abd al-Aziz had become strangely enigmatic. According to his physicians, the cause was melancholia, a malady that had afflicted him since childhood. More precisely, it began after an ornery mule gave him a swift kick, making a deep gash in his face that had left a permanent scar. For this reason, the treasurer had pinned his hopes on being able to choose the right time to appear before the caliph. The best time would clearly be one in which he was in a calm, agreeable mood. Unfortunately, no one had succeeded in finding him in a serene state of mind, nor could anyone say for certain what brought on his distress or annoyance. On the contrary, he had remained a riddle to all since occupying the caliphal residence. As his courtly retinue were all too aware, he was ever so dangerous!

The fiendish treasurer hovered around his benefactor for days, observing his facial expressions for clues to his emotional state, and attempting to read what lay hidden behind his gestures and behaviors. At the same time, he made a point of inquiring after the houscholds that had been ruined by his orders to wrest consorts from the arms of their masters and return them, along with their offspring, to their families in the Maghreb, until his quiver was filled to the brim with new tragedies bathed in sorrow. Then one day fortune smiled upon him when one of his co-conspirators approached him with the happy and unexpected news that thanks to the good offices of the Umayyad general Maslama ibn Abd al-Malik, the caliph had agreed to grant an audience to certain poets after a ban that had lasted an entire year or more. On that memorable day, the descendent of the righteous Umar ibn al-Khattab received a small group of bards which included Kuthayyar, Nusayb, and al-Ahwas.

After the caliph had debated with the visitors for some time, Kuthayyar implored him to listen to his recitation. Meanwhile, the treasurer lurked in the wings, hoping against hope that the poem would succeed in banishing the melancholia that had its grip on the ruler's heart. Pouring scorn on the things of this world while exalting abstinence and asceticism, the poet intoned:

249

The world has donned a harlot's garb
Brazenly flaunting her wiles
Her eyes ablaze with deceptive allure
And her mouth with pearly smiles.
Yet you turn away in loathing as though
She had mixed you a potion vile.

The lyrical tribute then reached its climax in the following stanza:

Ensconced in a mountainous fortress
From her storms you remain concealed
You shun the transient, though comely,
For the timeless with a will of steel.
You spurn the ephemeral, prepared
For a day of grim ordeal.

We are told by historians that, true to his insistence on truthfulness in all things, the caliph's parting words to Kuthayyar were, "God will hold you accountable for every word you have spoken!"

As al-Ahwas cleared his throat in a request for permission to recite, the caliph lowered his head in thought, then asked him to wait until he returned from performing the Friday prayer. Taking advantage of the caliph's absence, the treasurer took the chamberlain aside and explained to him that his delegation had come concerning a matter of urgency and needed to be granted a hearing without delay. His hope, of course, was that the poetry the caliph had heard in celebration of otherworldliness would drive the dark clouds from his soul before the next poet delivered his recitation.

57

The Pledge of Allegiance

DURING THE INTERLUDE BETWEEN THE two recitations, the caliph begrudgingly received the delegation. Opening the encounter, the treasurer began: "May the Commander of the Faithful pardon our haste. Were it not for our concern for the fate of the Umma, we would not have presumed upon him in this manner!"

The treasurer eyed the caliph as he lowered the mask of inscrutability over his features, then gazed into the distance as though he were searching the void for a prophecy.

"The fate of the Umma?"

The treasurer looked sharply at one of his Umayyad collaborators: a staid-looking elder, short of stature, his back so stooped that he leaned forward constantly, like someone on the verge of falling prostrate to kiss the ground. Tilting forward in pain, the man began, "The notables—"

Then he fell silent with a gulp.

"What about the notables?" the caliph prodded.

Rushing to his assistance, the treasurer cried, "They have raised a hue and cry, God keep the emir!"

"And why should they be raising a hue and cry?" demanded the caliph.

Drawing himself up, the other delegate exclaimed, "And how could they do otherwise—God keep the emir—when their affliction is too profound for words?"

The caliph shifted in his seat, a wary gleam in his eye.

At length he declared unequivocally, "If you are referring to those who wish to lord it over others, thinking that God is unaware of their evil deeds, they must reap what they have sown!"

The elderly man with the stooped back interjected, "But the punishment does not fit the crime!"

Casting the man a perplexed glance, the caliph stared back into the distance. After a pause, he asked, "So you're saying it isn't a crime to kidnap people's daughters and take them as wives—as paramours—at swordpoint?"

The second Umayyad delegate responded cunningly, "But once the ax has fallen, do we serve justice by virtue of a ruling that nullifies that which God has made permissible?"

Shooting him a stern look, the caliph replied ominously, "No act of coercion will ever be legitimate, and nothing can justify it even if a thousand axes have fallen!"

Leaping back into the fray, the stoop-backed elder reasoned, "Wouldn't fatwas issued by legal scholars help to set things right, God keep the emir?"

Hardly giving him time to finish his question, the caliph thundered, "What's right is right, and what's wrong is wrong, and the difference between them is clear as day!"

Silence fell over the hall. However, it was a silence so heavy that the treasurer rushed to break it, certain that if it continued, it would not bode well.

"However, God keep the emir, the harm we anticipate will not be due to returning concubines to their parents' embrace in an attempt to reverse the damage done by men's lust. Rather, the harm we fear will come from—"

He swallowed with difficulty before finishing his sentence. "The jizya!"

"The jizya?"

"Yes, God keep the emir!"

The treasurer fidgeted as Umar ibn Abd al-Aziz shot him a questioning look.

"If the emir might permit me to speak the truth, I would dare say that renouncing the jizya that has been imposed on the non-Arabs of North Africa will lead others to renounce their allegiance to you!"

"Renounce their allegiance?"

Emboldened by the look of astonishment on the caliph's face, one of the other delegates offered, "If the State Treasury were to be emptied, what would this entail, if not the loss of people's allegiance?"

After some hesitation, the caliph asked, "And why would the State Treasury become so empty that it would give people cause to renounce their allegiance?"

After exchanging another glance with the other delegation members, the treasurer declared, "Because the only thing that keeps the State Treasury full, God keep the emir, is the jizya imposed on the non-Arabs of Africa!"

The two men exchanged a long look during which the caliph didn't bat an eyelid. Seeing the gash in the Caliph's face grow suddenly longer and blacker, the treasurer closed his eyes and turned his gaze toward the floor. He remained in this position until the caliph growled, "If the ability to fill the State Treasury requires us to commit mortal sins against those who have uttered the two testimonies of faith, however distant the lands in which they dwell, then let it sit empty!"

As the treasurer locked eyes with his two companions, he detected a look of terror in their expressions. Shifting back and forth where he stood, he hastened to relieve their fear, saying, "God keep the emir—"

Interrupting him, the caliph roared, "If I were to forgive the governors for sacrificing our religion in exchange for indulging in what the religion has forbidden, the Almighty would never forgive me. Far be it from me to pardon them even if they rebel and renounce their allegiance to me. I, of all people, would be most entitled to renounce what you term 'allegiance', and I have no tolerance for fools who threaten to renounce their allegiance to me!"

58

The Pact

As the delegation members made their way back from the caliph's palace, the man with the stooped back said despondently, "Fatima bint Marwan spoke truly: We're reaping the bitter fruit of having leapt into the arms of the daughters of outsiders like Ibn al-Khattab simply because they were so alluring."

As the treasurer dragged his feet behind the other two men, looking like a defeated soldier on his way home from battle, he heard the other man reply, "Beauty is always a trap! Those who run after it are bound to slip and fall!"

Needing to catch their breath, the men entered a date palm grove in the center of which flowed an abundant spring. The hunchback paused to rest in the shade of a palm tree, while his companion fell asleep next to him. The treasurer stood over them, struggling to ward off a wicked thought that had begun eating away at him. The thought so terrified him that he dismissed it for fear that it might find its way to his lips, at which point he would be at its mercy. Hoping to shield himself from it, he lingered in the woods that encircled the spring.

Shortly after they reached the grove, the men were approached in haste by a young Umayyad. It was clear from his demeanor that he came bearing news. Panting, he told them that in a fit of rage, the caliph had dismissed the poets even before they finished their recitations. He added that after returning from the Friday prayer, the caliph had received a visit by an Umayyad delegation concerning some urgent matter. No sooner had the delegation departed than he turned on the poets, even threatening to throw them in prison if they didn't make themselves scarce.

The three conspirators exchanged glances for the hundredth time. This time, however, they were glances of a different kind. They watched the young man disappear behind the palm trees in search of some other ear eager to hear the grievous news he never tired of repeating.

The hunchback cast the treasurer a lengthy, inquisitive gaze as though he were discovering his presence among them for the first time. On his lips there flickered a cunning smile the meaning of which soon found its way to his tongue.

"I fear that his outburst was a result of what you said about allegiance."

The treasurer looked at him uncomprehendingly.

After some hesitation, the hunchback went on, "If you had said such a thing to Sulayman ibn Abd al-Malik ibn Marwan or to Abd al-Malik ibn Marwan, he would never have forgiven you for this blasphemy!"

Feeling a shudder go through his body as his saliva turned as bitter as colocynth, the treasurer murmured, "Might he actually have interpreted it as—?"

Then the hunchback said something that shook him to the core: "How could you threaten to renounce allegiance to the caliph?"

Clarifying the matter still further, the other companion added, "Mentioning the possibility of renouncing allegiance to a caliph in that caliph's very presence is a crime that could cost you your head!"

The treasurer felt the noose tightening around his throat.

Desperate to escape the horror of such a punishment, he objected, "But renouncing the right to collect the jizya from the people of Africa really *would* threaten the State Treasury with bankruptcy! If that should happen, there is a genuine threat that people would renounce—"

His saliva more bitter than ever now, he rattled, "their allegiance!"

"But how could you have dared utter such a thing in the caliph's hearing?" cried the hunchback.

Eyeing the treasurer with hostility, he continued, "Speaking in this way directly to the caliph was tantamount to urging others to renounce their allegiance to him. In fact, it was a threat to do so yourself. How can you oversee the State Treasury, yet be ignorant of this fact?"

The treasurer's mouth went dry. He didn't know what would have happened to him at that moment had he not been rescued by the iniquitous thought that had made its way into his consciousness a short while earlier, though he had initially fled from it in terror.

When the suggestion presented itself to him again, the color drained out of his face, and his forehead oozed with sweat. Nevertheless, he felt he had no choice but to test the waters.

He said, "I was risking my life in order to rescue your crumbling hold on power. If I failed because of a slip of the tongue, then you have no choice but to settle for the only antidote that remains to the House of the Umayyads."

A prolonged look charged with meaning—indeed, with numerous meanings— passed among the three men. His heart suddenly pierced through by the treasurer's oblique statement, the hunchback leapt to his feet.

"Do you mean what you're saying?" he asked, his eyes darting back and forth between the two other men.

"I have nothing to lose," the treasurer replied. "And don't forget," he added after a pause. "This is the only solution that remains to you if you want to maintain your power!"

The hunchback drew up to the treasurer until, thanks to his involuntary forward tilt, the two men's heads touched, and the treasurer could feel the man's breath against his face.

At length the hunchback hissed, "Can you take care of this matter on our behalf?"

Glancing over at their other companion, the treasurer found him looking back at him with a curious gleam in his eye. Turning his gaze again to the hunchback, he contemplated him at length before whispering, "Yes, I can. But as you might guess, the proof of the pudding will be in the eating."

The hunchback exchanged a questioning look with his companion, who gestured a request for clarification.

Explaining himself, the treasurer said, "I don't need money. If I did, I wouldn't be the treasurer! Your role will come in after it's over because, although I may be able to spare you the tribulation that has afflicted us all so suddenly, I can't guarantee that no one will be suspicious of you. After all, fools are bound to gossip."

"Don't worry. If you do the job well, no one will butt heads over it. As the noble Prophet said, 'If any of you does a job, God wants you to do it well!'"

After a silence, the treasurer smiled, saying, "There's no need to ask whether I will do the job well or not. All I ask is that you protect me from your fellow Umayyads. As for the citizenry, leave them to me!"

The hunchback murmured, "You might have reason to doubt the position of the Umayyads if they themselves hadn't been the victims of the caliph's policies!"

The three men stared at each other without a word until the treasurer broke the silence.

"Is this a pact?" he asked.

Neither of the other two men replied. However, without hesitation they each took two steps toward the treasurer and placed their hands in his. At that moment, the twilight immersed the crowns of the palm trees in a crimson glow as though the sky had begun to bleed.

59

The Antidote

SEVERAL DAYS AFTER THE TRIPARTITE gathering, on the sixth day of Shaaban, AH 101/723 CE, people awoke to the voice of the herald as he announced the passing of the Commander of the Faithful, Umar ibn Abd al-Aziz, descendent of the wise and discerning Umar ibn al-Khattab. Forty-one years of age at the time, his inescapable end had overtaken him on the morning of that day due to a sudden illness. The youngest of all the Umayyad caliphs, he had served in the caliphate for a mere two years and five months, the shortest reign of any Umayyad ruler.

It was as though the Fates had determined to teach the generations a lesson in division and justice, namely, that the shares of history allotted to justice are but pitiful respites during which it pays us fleeting visits, alighting briefly as a phantom in the lower realms of creation. Yet it is a small, time-bound exception to a crushing rule: that injustice alone reigns immortal!

Key Terms

Abd al-Malik ibn Marwan ibn al-Hakam (644–705 CE): A member of the first generation of born Muslims, Abd al-Malik ibn Marwan was the fifth Umayyad caliph, in which capacity he ruled from 685 till his death in 705.

Abdullah ibn Abi Sarh (d. 656 CE): The milk-brother of Uthman ibn Affan, who appointed him Governor of Egypt to replace Amr ibn al-As in the year 646 CE. He is said to have left Islam during the lifetime of the Prophet due to his belief that he could anticipate Quranic verses not yet revealed. The Prophet wanted him executed, but Uthman interceded on his behalf and the penalty was not carried out. He is reported to have returned to Islam at the conquest of Mecca.

Abdullah ibn al-Zubayr (624–92 CE): Abdullah ibn al-Zubayr headed a caliphate in Mecca which rivaled that of the Umayyads from 683 CE until his death in 692 CE. He was killed by Hajjaj ibn Yusuf on orders from the Umayyad caliph Abd al-Malik ibn Marwan.

Abu Dharr al-Ghifari (d. 652 CE): A prominent Companion of the Prophet Muhammad known for his piety, asceticism, and concern for the poor.

Amazigh: The language of the Berbers. A sister to ancient Egyptian, Amazigh is the language in which the Stone of Massinissa was inscribed.

Barca: From the Arabic *barqa*, meaning "the road." The word *barqa* also means "road" in the ancient Libyan tongue and is still used in this sense among the Tuaregs.

Battle of Jalula': Fought in 637 CE in Jalula', a strategic town which constituted the gate to northern Iraq, between the forces of Caliph Umar ibn al-Khattab and those of the Persian Sassanid Empire. The Muslim victory at Jalula' led to the Muslim takeovers of Tikrit and Mosul as well.

Buturs: The Butur tribes from which the Priestess Dahiya was descended represent the nomadic portion of the Berber people who had settled throughout North Africa and the Great Desert. More specifically, the Butur belong to the group of people known as the Tuareg. One possible etymology of the word Tuareg is that it is the broken plural of the Arabic adjective *targi* (from Targa, the name of a region rich in springs and lakes in the south of Libya, present-day Fezzan).

al-furqan: Meaning "proof," "evidence," or "that which distinguishes right from wrong and truth from falsehood," the term *al-furqan* is typically used to refer to the Quran.

Fustat: Fustat was the first capital of Egypt under Muslim rule, established by General Amr ibn al-As after the Muslim conquest of Egypt in 641 CE.

Garamantes: Encompassing various Berber tribes, the Garamantes founded a number of kingdoms or city-states between roughly 500 BC and 700 CE in the Fezzan area of Libya.

Hajjaj ibn Yusuf (661–714 CE): A governor of Iraq, known for his severity, who was appointed by Caliph Abd al-Malik ibn Marwan (r. 685–705 CE).

Hanash Sanaani: Following the slaying of Uqba ibn Nafi at the hands of Byzantine-backed Berbers led by Kusaila in 683, panic ensued among the Arab troops of Kairouan; the majority sided with Hanash Sanaani, who advocated for withdrawal to Barca (Cyrenaica), while Zuhayr ibn Qays al-Balawi favored resistance. The army ultimately withdrew.

Hassan ibn al-Nu'man (d. 705 CE): Appointed by Caliph Abd al-Malik ibn Marwan, Ibn al-Nu'man led the final Muslim conquest of Ifriqiya, firmly establishing Islamic rule in the region through a series of campaigns in which he defeated the Byzantines and the Berbers led by al-Kahina. He was ultimately ousted from his post by the Governor of Egypt, Abd al-Aziz ibn Marwan.

houris: In Islamic religious belief, *houris* are beautiful, wide-eyed maidens who will accompany faithful Muslim believers in Paradise.

Idkran: Idkran was the chief of desert tribes whose territory bordered on Libya's coastal region, and with whom Greek settlers concluded a non-aggression pact allowing the settlers to remain within the coastal region. However, unable to resist the temptation to encroach inland in their quest for the magical silphium plant, which was considered a panacea for all ills (and which ancient Greek monarchs considered so valuable that they monopolized the right to trade in it), the Greeks violated the non-aggression pact. In their effort to force the Greeks back to the coast, the Libyans sought the assistance of the pharaohs in neighboring Egypt. There ensued a fierce war which the Libyans lost to the Greeks. However, Idkran (whose name in the Tuareg language means "rage") later distanced himself from the Egyptians and went on to inflict a historic defeat on the Greeks, which cost them seven thousand troops. In the aforementioned war, Idkran sought the assistance of the Garamantes, the most powerful of all the desert tribes at that time, and successfully forced the Greek settlers to withdraw once more to the coast.

Ismail ibn Abi al-Muhajir: Ismail ibn Abi al-Muhajir served as governor over North Africa between 718–20 CE under the caliphate of Umar ibn Abd al-Aziz.

jizya: The jizya is a tax imposed on non-Muslim subjects of a Muslim state.

Jugurtha (160–104 BC): The Berber monarch of Numidia (present-day Constantine, Algeria) from 118–105 BC, Jugurtha led devastating guerrilla campaigns against the Romans. After being betrayed by his father-in-law to Roman commander Gaius Marius, Jugurtha was taken captive and severely mistreated, and is said to have starved to death in a Roman prison.

al-Kahina (d. 703 CE): A Berber queen, priestess, and military leader who succeeded the Berber king Kusaila in leading indigenous resistance to the Muslim conquest of the Maghreb, the region then known as Numidia. Although her personal name was Dahiya (or Daya, Dehiya, Dihya, or Dahya), which may possibly be derived from the Arabic *dahiya*, meaning, "the Cunning One," Arabic-language sources identify her as al-Kahina (the priestess soothsayer) given her alleged ability to foresee the future. According to some accounts, Dahiya died fighting the invaders, sword in hand. Other accounts say she committed suicide by swallowing poison rather than be taken by the enemy.

Kusaila (d. 688 CE): Kusaila was a seventh-century Berber ruler of the Kingdom of Altava, and leader of the Berber Awraba tribe. Kusaila died in the year 688 at the Battle of Mamma, fighting the Muslims under the command of Umayyad General Zuhayr ibn Qays al-Balawi.

Lamtuna: The Lamtuna were a nomadic Berber tribe belonging to the Sanhaja (Zenaga) confederation whose horsemen formed the nucleus of the Almoravid Empire (1040–47 CE) in present-day Morocco led by the Tuareg Yusuf ibn Tashfin (1009–1106 CE). At the height of its power, the Almoravid Empire extended as far south as Guinea and Ghana, and northward into Spain and the Balearic Islands.

Massinissa (238–148 BC): With Roman support, Massinissa united the eastern and western Numidian tribes and founded the Kingdom of Numidia.

Muawiya (r. 661–680 CE): The first Umayyad caliph.

Musa ibn Nusayr (640–716 CE): As Governor of North Africa under the Umayyad caliph al-Walid I, Musa ibn Nusayr ruled over the Muslim provinces of North Africa (Ifriqiya) and directed the Islamic conquest of the Visigothic Kingdom in Hispania (present-day Portugal, Spain, Andorra, and part of France).

The North: A reference to the region north of the Great Desert, where Berber tribes who had chosen a non-nomadic lifestyle established themselves. This is the region that witnessed the establishment of ancient civilizations such as that of the Phoenicians in Carthage (present-day Tunisia) in the ninth century BC, a Greek civilization established in the seventh century BC centered in Cyrenaica (eastern Libya), and the Roman civilization that grew up in Sabratha and elsewhere in western Libya (146 BC–672 CE).

rebab: A rebab is a bowed (sometimes plucked) string instrument that has existed in various sizes and shapes, and which spread via Islamic trading routes over much of North Africa, Southeast Asia, the Middle East, and parts of Europe.

Roman Sea: An earlier name for the body of water now termed the Mediterranean Sea. It was referred to by ancient inhabitants of Europe as Mare Libycom (Latin for "the Libyan Sea").

Tanit: The Goddess Tanit was the mother deity of Carthage, protector of the city and provider of fertility. As such, she seems to have been a deity of good fortune. Goddess of the heavens, she was often associated with the moon. Many stone slabs from that area feature the so-called Sign of Tanit, which resembles a stylized human body formed by a triangle topped with a circle, the two shapes being separated by a horizontal line with or without upturned ends. See https://phoenicia.org/pagan.html.

Thouda: Also referred to as Tahuda or Tabuda (former Roman Thabudeos), the ruins of Thouda are located in present-day Biskra in northeastern Algeria. It was in Thouda that, in the year 683 CE, the Berber king Kusaila ambushed and killed the Umayyad general Uqba ibn Nafi during the latter's return from a campaign he had led across North Africa.

Umar ibn Abd al-Aziz (682–720 CE): The most just and pious of the Umayyad caliphs (reigned 717–20 CE), Umar ibn Abd al-Aziz has been dubbed the fifth of the rightly guided caliphs.

Uqba ibn Nafi (622–83 CE): Uqba ibn Nafi commanded the Arab army that occupied Tunisia in 670 and led a Muslim invasion across North Africa as far as the Atlantic Ocean.

Before his recall in 674, Uqba founded the city of Kairouan (in present-day Tunisia), which became the first center of Arab administration in the Maghreb. In 683 CE, on his way back from his expedition, Uqba was ambushed and killed by a Berber–Byzantine coalition led by Kusaila at Thouda, south of Vescera. Following the crushing defeat suffered by Uqba's army, the Arabs were expelled from the area of modern-day Tunisia and Algeria for over a decade, and his army retreated to Barca.

Valley of the Virgins: The site of the Battle of Meskiana, this encounter took place in 698 CE. The battle site is referred to as "the Valley of the Virgins" in sympathy for the young women whose potential husbands were lost in great numbers in the fighting.

Zuhayr ibn Qays al-Balawi (d. 688 CE): When the province known as Ifriqiya (comprising parts of modern-day Algeria, Tunisia, and Libya) fell to a Byzantine–Berber alliance in 682 CE, Zuhayr was appointed by Caliph Abd al-Malik ibn Marwan to lead a campaign to retake the territory. To that end, Zuhayr recaptured Kairouan, the Arabs' capital in Ifriqiya, and drove the Berbers west to the Valley of Mamma, where he slew Berber chief Kusaila in 688 CE. In that same year, however, Uqba was slain by Byzantine raiders on his way back to Barca (Cyrenaica).

Notes

1 The "two confessions" refers to the dual testimony by which one enters Islam: "I bear witness that there is no god but God, and Muhammad is the Messenger of God."

2 "The most distant deserts" refers to the stretch of desert extending through the Sahara southward to the frontiers of the African jungles in the area near Timbuktu (present-day Mali) and Agadez (present-day Niger).

3 The amulet mentioned is a metaphorical reference to the rites of brotherhood described in the next chapter.

4 The word "Quran" is derived from the Arabic verb *qara'a,* meaning "to read."

5 "Sacred foods" is a reference to a rite of bonding among certain Berber tribes whose sacred foods consisted of barley flour mixed with breast milk.

6 This magic ritual, which was prevalent in the era in which the events of the novel are set, is still practiced today.

7 A reference to *Surat al-Baqara* 2:256, which reads, "Let there be no compulsion in religion: Truth stands out clear from error: whoever rejects evil and believes in God hath grasped the most trustworthy hand-hold that never breaks. And God heareth and knoweth all things."

SELECTED HOOPOE TITLES

Gold Dust
by Ibrahim al-Koni, translated by Elliott Colla

I Do Not Sleep
by Ihsan Abdel Kouddous, translated by Jonathan Smolin

Here is a Body
by Basma Abdel Aziz, translated by Jonathan Wright

*

hoopoe is an imprint for engaged, open-minded readers hungry for outstanding fiction that challenges headlines, re-imagines histories, and celebrates original storytelling. Through elegant paperback and digital editions, **hoopoe** champions bold, contemporary writers from across the Middle East alongside some of the finest, groundbreaking authors of earlier generations.

At hoopoefiction.com, curious and adventurous readers from around the world will find new writing, interviews, and criticism from our authors, translators, and editors.

CPSIA information can be obtained
at www.ICGtesting.com
Printed in the USA
LVHW111203020123
736145LV00034B/502/J